EMPRESS IN LINGERIE

Lingerie #5

PENELOPE SKY

Hartwick Publishing

Copyright © 2018 by Penelope Sky

Contents

Vanessa

THE LAST TWO WEEKS HAD BEEN BUSY.

I caught up on my school work, finished the painting I was working on, and finally transformed my apartment so it didn't contain the scent of the man who took me hostage.

Knuckles.

What kind of name was that?

Sapphire and I texted almost every day, and she told me she and my brother were still finalizing their wedding plans. They wanted to do something small at the house, just family and lots of wine.

I loved both of those things, so I was down.

When I went to the market the other day, I ran into a handsome guy who reached for the same box of cereal. We exchanged a few words, and it turned out, he didn't even like that brand of cereal. He just wanted an excuse to find out what my name was.

Then we went to dinner. Anytime a guy asked me out, I always insisted we meet at a casual café. Big, romantic dinners were overrated and just awkward. I didn't want a man to try to impress me by buying me an expensive meal. Wealth wasn't impressive to me. I wanted a man who was all man, someone who couldn't hide behind money or success.

His name was Tony, and he was nice enough. He worked at an investment firm, taking people's savings and putting it in the stock market. He was young for that line of work, and it sounded like it was his first year working there.

The date was pleasant but nothing special.

It was never special.

Sometimes I met a guy and we really hit it off, but then the chemistry didn't go beyond sex. We just got off on each other and enjoyed passionate nights of good and sweaty sex. But there was nothing substantial there, so I stopped calling. Then he stopped calling.

And then it was like it never happened.

But this guy didn't do anything for me, so at the end of the night, I paid my half of the bill, said good-night, and then walked home.

After the incident with Knuckles, I was a lot more paranoid than I used to be. How did he figure out where I was living? Did he follow me on my way home? Or did he simply do some research online? Whatever the answer was, I always took a different route home, just in case I was being followed.

When I turned the corner and walked down the quiet street, it began to snow. Small flakes floated from the sky, and the white color contrasted against the darkness of the evening. I stopped to let one touch the tip of my nose. I let it melt before I kept going. I preferred the heat of summer, but I still thought the winters in northern Italy were gorgeous. When the streets were blanketed with snow, it was a sight to behold. It was a pain to walk in it on the way to class, but it was still beautiful to see.

I stopped again when I heard a sound I would never forget.

A guttural sound, like someone drowning in their own blood.

The thud of a dead body hitting the ground.

And then the smack of a pipe cracking someone's skull.

I stopped and turned my gaze down the dark alleyway, even though I knew there was nothing I wanted to see. That's when I saw the dark outline of a man looming over a corpse on the ground. The victim had just died, so the freezing temperatures hadn't turned his warm body cold yet. The shadow hid the stranger's face, but he was the size of a monster. Tall, muscular, and large, he made Knuckles look pathetic.

I quickly faced forward again and kept walking, not wanting the monster to know I'd just witnessed a murder.

A fucking murder.

It happened so fast I didn't think to call the police. I didn't have a knife or a weapon to intervene. But I knew it would be stupid to put myself in harm's way when I didn't even know what was going on.

They could have been two homeless men fighting over a dumpster.

It wasn't even nine in the evening yet, but there was no one out because of the cold.

Why did I have to be the only one out there?

I didn't hear a single sound, so there was no way for me to anticipate what would happen next. I had a strong instinct and could feel things around me before I saw or felt them. But this guy was no average man, and he snuck up on me without his boots crunching against the snow.

His hand slapped against my mouth, and he silenced me before I could even scream.

Then the knife came. The steel blade was ice-cold against my throat. He pressed it hard into me, telling me he meant business. His voice was cold like the knife, icy like the air burning my lungs. The snow started to fall harder now, blocking my view of the nearest apartment building. It was the perfect coverage for something like this. "Make a sound, and I'll slit your throat. I'll let you bleed out like a pig at the slaughter."

Why didn't I just take a different route home? I took another deep breath but remained still.

"Good girl."

I hated that phrase. I detested it every time a man used it. It was insulting, belittling, and sexist. I spoke against his hand. "Fuck. You."

"What did I just—"

I stomped on his foot and tried to roll him forward the way my father taught me, but this guy was the size of an ox, and all I did was jerk him a little. I abandoned the attempt and tried to run for it.

"Stupid. Fucking. Girl." He snatched my ankle and pulled so I fell forward onto the concrete. He came at me with the knife again, this time to make good on his word. He moved on top of me, ready to plunge it into my throat so I couldn't scream for help.

But then his eyes flashed over my face. There was an instant of emotion, a look of familiarity. It was the first time I could see his face—his fair skin, bright blue eyes, and his chiseled jawline. I imagined my attacker to be dirty, homeless, and gross.

Not gorgeous.

Not manly.

Not…handsome as hell.

He continued to grip the knife, but something

stopped him from making good on his threat. I knew he was going to do it, saw the blood lust in his eyes. He wasn't the kind of man to make empty threats.

Something changed his mind.

He shoved the knife into the sheath then lifted me over his shoulder.

That's when I started to scream for help. I screamed at the top of my lungs, begging someone to hear me beyond the snow fall. Someone had to be home in one of the nearby apartments. Someone would report this to the police.

The man carried me down the alleyway toward a black van parked near the dumpster. "Scream all you want. By the time someone hears you and actually thinks to act on it, we'll be long gone. And if by some miracle the police actually arrive, they'll take one look at me and turn the other way." He set me on the ground, right on top of a pile of snow. With lightning speed, he pulled a gun out of his pocket and pointed it in my face.

I stopped screaming, abandoning my call for help. I had to think of something to do—and do it quickly.

The corner of his mouth rose in a smile, and his eyes

squinted with interest. "Why did you stop screaming?"

"Because I'm trying to figure out how to kill you."

The half-smile he wore quickly turned into a full grin. A small chuckle even escaped his lips. He pressed the barrel to my cheek, the cool metal freezing like the snow. "You're cute." He got off me then holstered his gun, like he wasn't the least bit afraid of me.

He shouldn't underestimate me.

He even turned his back on me as he walked to the corpse he left behind. "Don't run. It'll be a lot worse in the end." He grabbed the man by the ankles and dragged him across the asphalt and snow. He purposely set the man right next to me.

I'd never stared at a dead person before. I shot that guy when I was escaping Knuckles, but I didn't stop to examine him. This guy was mutilated, his skull crushed in until his face was hardly recognizable.

I felt vomit rise in my throat.

The man kneeled down so we were eye level. There was a shadow underneath his jaw because his bone structure was so chiseled. He had a sprinkle of hair there, thick enough to cover his skin but not thick enough to be a beard. His fair skin complemented the brightness of his eyes. With dirty blond hair, he looked like a man who belonged on a magazine cover rather than in an alleyway in Milan. He wore a black leather jacket, black jeans, and brown boots. No amount of clothing could hide what was underneath his attire. He was strong, muscular, and powerful. "You don't want to end up like that, right?"

I couldn't look at the dead man again, terrorized by what I just saw. "You don't either. So I suggest you let me go."

He chuckled, the light reaching his eyes. Even though the laugh was full of amusement, it seemed sarcastic. Regardless of what expression he wore, he was undeniably handsome. Why the hell was a guy like this murdering people? "I can't remember the last time someone made me laugh."

"I don't think there's anything funny about your own death."

He smiled again then grabbed a body bag from the van.

I stared down the alleyway and thought of running. I was fast, but this man was faster. If I saw someone pass in the alleyway, I would sprint for it. Or maybe I could dig my phone out of my purse. It was still with me.

I only had a second to decide.

I went for the phone. I tried to be discreet as I unzipped the zipper.

He returned with the body bag and rolled the man inside. He didn't look at me as he guessed what I was doing. "I'm telling you, the cops won't touch me. So you better call someone good."

My father was too far away. Even Conway was too far away. But I had to do something.

He carried the grown man into the back of the van and dropped him with a loud thud.

I yanked my purse open and immediately stuck my hand inside to grab my phone.

He snatched the purse out of my hand and threw it in the back of the van. "You're slow."

"Fuck you," I hissed.

Like everything else, my words amused him. "Get in the passenger seat. Or I'll put you in the passenger seat."

I eyed the van then faced forward again, looking at the street.

"Baby, don't even think about it." He shook his head slightly. "You won't get far. And when you do get caught, the punishment will be severe."

"Don't call me baby."

"You're my baby now," he said. "I can call you whatever I damn well please."

"You're going to kill me anyway." I rose to my feet and dusted off the snow. "So I may as well—" I took off at a dead sprint, running for my life. I had to get to the street. I had to get out of there. If I got into that van, I would never see the light of day again. I would much rather die trying to escape than let him rape me then carve me with a knife.

I didn't even make it halfway when his large hand grabbed my shoulder, and he shoved a taser into my neck. He shocked me at full intensity, making my entire body go rigid before I collapsed. I hit the asphalt, slightly disoriented by the electrocution. But I didn't let myself stay down. I didn't allow myself to be weak. I pushed up and started to run again.

This time, he laughed louder. "Jesus Christ, I've never

seen that before." He caught up to me again, and this time, he zapped me for twice as long. He hit me on the other side of the neck, making a new scar.

I collapsed again, feeling weaker than I did last time. I just wanted to lie there. I just wanted to give up. This guy was beyond my skills. He was a powerhouse. My small size inhibited me completely.

He stood over me. "Now, *baby*. It's time to get in the van."

I didn't care if the fight wasn't fair. I didn't care if this induced a heart attack. I'd crawl to the street if I had to. "Fuck. Off." My arms shook as I pushed myself to my feet. I stumbled forward as my legs failed to carry me. I was too weak, but that didn't stop me from moving my body forward.

He whistled. "Alright, I admit it. I'm impressed. I've taken down grown ass men twice your size with this thing." He slowly followed me, watching me crawl.

My fingers dug into the asphalt as I kept crawling. If I just stalled long enough, someone would show up.

"I'll do it again, baby. But this time, it might kill you."

"I'd rather die on the ground as a fighter than surrender to a piece of shit like you."

This time, he stopped following me. He stared at me, watching me crawl away.

I didn't know what he was thinking. I didn't know if that pissed him off or impressed him. I didn't have time to care. I had to focus all my energy on moving.

Lights reflected off the buildings, and then I heard the sirens.

Thank fucking god. "I'm here!"

A cop car pulled up to the alleyway, and an officer got out of the driver's seat. With his gun drawn, he was ready to take out my captor.

But the officer hesitated. He took one look at my captor, lowered his gun, and then got back in the car.

"No!" I pushed myself to my knees and waved my arm. "Help me!"

The cop drove away.

"No!" I watched his taillights until they disappeared. And like no one had been there at all, the street returned to silence.

The man came up behind me, his knees hitting my back. His hand wrapped around my neck, and he forced my chin up, making me meet his gaze. He didn't stare down at me in victory. It actually seemed like he pitied me.

Then he shoved a needle into my neck.

And I was gone.

————

WHEN I WOKE UP, I was sitting in the passenger seat of the van with my cheek pressed to the cold window. The ride was bumpy, like we were driving over rough terrain. My mind was still foggy, and I could have kept sleeping, but when I remembered my position and the man who took me, I snapped out of it.

My eyes opened, and I looked out the window to see a line of trees covered in snow. It was still snowing and pitch-black outside. Now we were in the middle of nowhere, away from the city.

Away from people.

Shit.

My hands weren't bound and neither were my ankles.

There was some hope.

I tried to pretend I was still sleeping. That way, I could catch him by surprise. It was a stupid idea, but I could take the wheel and turn the van off the road. I might break an arm or something, but he also might die.

That would be nice.

His deep voice filled the air. "I know you're awake, baby." The radio wasn't on, and only the sounds of the moving van filled our ears. The dead guy in the back rolled from side to side when we turned. I could hear the tap of my purse too.

I wished I could reach my purse. "Where are we?"

"Lake Garda."

North of Verona. That meant we passed Conway's home on the drive, along with Carter's. Shit, why didn't I just stay with them longer to recover? And why did I have to go on that date? If I'd just taken a different route last night, I wouldn't be on my way to a freezing lake where he would dump my body. "I'm not letting you drown me in that lake."

He chuckled, amused once again. "I don't think you're in any position to call the shots."

"For now," I said ominously. "But I assure you, I will be."

Each corner of his mouth rose in a wide grin. "I've never had a prisoner more amusing. They usually cry for a while. Then they start begging. They never fight back. But you're an anomaly."

"Because you don't want to mess with me."

"Ironic," he said. "You don't want to mess with me either." He finally turned his head my way, his handsome expression hard but amused. He turned back to the road, his sculpted jawline so hard it looked like someone cut it out with a knife. Men that handsome weren't supposed to be serial killers. He could have had a much different life if he wanted to.

"Why are you doing this?"

"Need to be more specific, baby."

Ugh, I hated that word. I hated the way it fell on my ears. "Why are you killing innocent men in dark alleyways?"

"Why do you assume he's innocent?" he countered. "He could be even more evil than I am."

"Because you took me. And I'm pretty sure I'm as innocent as they come."

He started to smile again. "You were in the wrong place at the wrong time. Innocent or not, I can't let you get away."

"Why?" I demanded. "The police are afraid of you. So who could I tell?"

His hand tightened on the steering wheel, and he stared out the front window. The edges of the windows were frosted with ice, and even though the defroster was on, it couldn't combat the freezing temperatures. "I know who you are, Vanessa Barsetti. There are worse people you could tell."

My blood suddenly turned ice-cold, colder than the snow outside. I'd been scared this entire time, but now my terror reached a new level. I'd hoped he'd let me go because I was an innocent nobody. But now that he knew who I was, there was no going back. If he let me go and I told my family, they would hunt him until there was nothing left of him. The odds of repercussions were too great. The Barsetti family was far more formidable than the entire police force. He must have looked at my ID in my purse when I was passed out and recognized my last name.

My heart started to beat harder, and despite how cold it was, my palms got sweaty. Even if I could reach my phone right now, I probably had no reception.

Fuck, this was bad.

I'd just escaped Knuckles a month ago, and now I was being taken again. But this time, my opponent was far more terrifying and intelligent. The attempts I made to evade my captor last time wouldn't work now.

But that didn't mean I wouldn't try.

My father was so proud of me when I escaped. The emotion was in his eyes like never before.

I had to make him proud again.

I threw my hands across the center console and grabbed the wheel, determined to make it crash into a pile of snow or a tree. I pushed the steering wheel to the left, but his grip was too tight.

He slammed his foot on the gas, pushing the van at top speed. Then he turned his face toward me, his look so intense it resembled the underworld. With only a single hand, he managed to keep the steering wheel straight. He let the van fly down the icy road as he mocked me with his gaze. He challenged me, unafraid of the unknown ahead of us.

I yanked on the steering wheel again, but his grip was too tight. Now we were going ninety down the icy road, and if I didn't back off, we would both be killed when we slammed head first into a tree.

His blue eyes were malicious, unflinching with a lack of fear. Death didn't scare him. He'd rather make sure the crash killed both of us than risk my getting away. "Let go or we both die."

A guarantee of death would defeat the purpose of this. So I let go and returned to my seat.

He lifted his foot off the gas.

He slowed us down before we came to a bend in the road. He turned into the curve and kept the van from spinning out of control. Then, like nothing happened at all, we cruised down the path with the piles of snow on either side.

I pressed my forehead against the window and sighed. "Fuck."

"I admire your bravery. But I don't admire your stupidity."

I kept my gaze out the window. "Let me go, and I promise I won't say anything to my family. We'll pretend it never happened. You don't want to be in this situation. If they figure out it was you who killed me, they'll never stop until you and your whole family are dead."

"Well, they already killed my family, so that's one less thing on the list…"

I turned my head back to him. "What?"

He stared straight ahead. "And I don't care if they come after me. It'll give me an opportunity to kill the rest. So, no, letting you go isn't an option. I want them to know I killed you. I want them to suffer. Letting you go would rob me of my vengeance. Trust me, I'm going to kill you. I just have to make it good."

"But you came across me by accident."

"Was it on accident?" he said quietly.

My skin pebbled with bumps. "What did my family do to you? They're peaceful people. You must be confused."

"No." He slowed down when he reached a turn in the road. He went right and headed down the weathered path. "I'm definitely not confused." The tires crunched over the snow as we approached the beach at the lake. The water wasn't frozen, but at this time of year, the peaks around it were covered with snow. Tourists flocked here every summer, but in the winter, it was abandoned.

There would be no one for miles. My screams wouldn't make a difference. "What about the man in the back? Was he just in the wrong place at the wrong time?"

"I wouldn't worry about him. You're still alive, so I would worry about yourself right now." He killed the engine then hopped out of the van.

My breathing increased, and I started to panic. I could usually keep my cool even in the worst circumstances, but now that there was no hope, I really felt like my death was imminent. My parents loved me so much, and they would never get over my death. My brother would be devastated too, along with the rest of my family. I didn't want them to suffer. Even if he drowned me in the ice-cold lake, I wouldn't suffer as much as they would.

Think, Vanessa.

He opened the backdoor to the van and dragged out the body of his first victim.

I turned in my seat to look at him. "What are you doing?"

"Throwing him in the lake." He dragged the body over the ground then across the snow toward the water. The keys to the van were in his pocket, so I couldn't take off. My father never taught me how to hot-wire a car, but I yanked open the compartment underneath the steering wheel and tried. There were lots of wires, and I couldn't figure out what to cut and what not to cut. I ripped them all out just to be spiteful. After he killed me, I hoped his engine wouldn't start. Maybe he would freeze to death out here.

Served him right.

When I leaned over, I noticed a small piece of metal under his seat. I glanced out the window to see him dragging the body to the end of the pier. He was almost to the end where he would push the corpse into the lake.

I turned back and grabbed the metal.

It was a gun.

A fucking gun.

Yes.

I sat upright and checked the barrel.

One bullet.

I couldn't miss.

The man kicked the corpse into the water then turned around. He walked back toward me.

Now that I had some hope in my veins, my hands wouldn't stop shaking. This moment was about life or death. If I didn't aim perfectly and hit him right in the heart or the skull, I would blow my only chance.

I wasn't going to miss.

I waited until he was close to the van before I opened the door and got out. I kept the gun hidden at my side so he wouldn't notice it right away.

He was at least six-three, tall and muscular. He was packed with muscle on muscle, and he held himself with a formidable posture at all times. His blue eyes may have been pretty, but they were terrifying. His look was trained on me, an omen of what would come next. "Your turn, baby."

"Don't call me baby." I aimed the gun and pointed it right at his heart. I didn't hesitate to look for the terror in his eyes. I didn't give myself any time to think about anything. I just had to kill this guy.

I pulled the trigger.

I missed his heart, but I hit him in the shoulder.

His body jerked slightly with the momentum of the bullet, but not once did his expression change. He didn't show pain or fear. Like he was receiving a shot at the doctor's office, it was just a quick pinch.

He halted in his tracks as he stared at me, and his furious expression changed into a different look altogether. Intense, territorial, and frightening, he looked at me like I was his next victim. His chest rose and fell at a quicker rate, the adrenaline spiking in his blood.

I still had the gun, so I had something to whack him with.

But he had a gun too. It sat on his hip. All he had to do was pull it out and snuff out my life right then and there.

But he didn't.

He stormed me, moving at a quick pace over the snow and heading right for me.

I raised the gun to smack him in the skull.

Without looking at it, he grabbed my wrist and smashed it against the side of the van, forcing my fingers to release the butt of the gun. It fell to the snow as my body was pressed against the door of the van.

One hand moved into my hair, and he crushed his mouth to mine.

And kissed me.

He kissed me aggressively, like he'd been wanting to do it for the last few hours and finally gave in. His massive body pressed against me, and he breathed warm air into my lungs. It was silent outside, the echo of the gunshot long gone.

He felt my lips with his own, sucking my bottom lip before he migrated to the top. His mouth worked mine, taking the lead and cherishing me like a man madly in love with a woman. There was more passion in that embrace than any other man had ever shown me. His cock was hard in his jeans, and I could feel it press against me.

It was a monster, just like he was.

It happened so fast I didn't have time to think about what I was doing. But I kissed him back, my body naturally following his. I'd never been kissed this way, with such masculine possession. This man didn't give me a chance to decide what I wanted. He just took me, like he already owned me.

Blood seeped from his wound and dripped down his leather jacket. It got on my jacket and my fingertips, warm in the frigid temperatures. He was bleeding badly, but that didn't deter him from giving me the best kiss of my life. It didn't stop the blood from giving him a huge hard-on.

I'd never met a man like this.

He fisted my hair harder, taking charge by force. His tongue came next, slipping into my mouth and meeting mine.

My tongue danced with his, the seductive embrace making me forget the cold.

Packed with heat, desperation, and chemistry, the kiss was exceptional. It had to be under the circumstances.

Then he abruptly ended it, pulling his warm mouth away and leaving me exposed to the cold air once more. "Get your ass in the van." He snatched the empty gun from the ground and got into the driver's seat.

My back was still to the door as I considered what just happened. I was still breathing hard, processing the euphoric moment I just felt. I shot the guy with the intention to kill.

And his response was to kiss me.

The engine roared to life.

Did that mean he wasn't going to kill me?

He honked the horn.

I snapped out of it and got into the passenger seat. I buckled my safety belt and watched the clearing disappear as we headed back to the road. "Does that mean you aren't going to kill me?"

He pulled onto the main road but didn't turn back the way we came. "Oh, I'm definitely going to kill you."

2

Bones

VANESSA BARSETTI.

With gorgeous black hair and Italian olive skin, she was a beauty. Her green eyes contrasted against her exotic features, making them astounding and expressive. When I was about to butcher her on the sidewalk with a knife, I got a glimpse of her features in the darkness.

And I recognized her.

I didn't plan it, but she fell right into my lap. I didn't believe in destiny or fate.

But I believed in karma.

She came to me for a reason, walked past that alleyway because she was supposed to.

That way, I could take her and do what needed to be done.

The blood war had never ended. It was simply paused.

I drove down the dark road then turned left, away from the lake. I began the windy ascent to the top of the mountain, to a piece of property I bought a long time ago. There wasn't another house in sight, and since the terrain was difficult to scale, it was the perfect hideaway for my criminal activities.

I drove twenty minutes up the snowy mountain with Vanessa silent beside me. I told her I was going to kill her, and I meant it. She should enjoy her last minutes of life as best she could, because she didn't have a lot of time left.

I just had to decide the perfect way to kill her.

To make it hurt.

Drowning her in a frozen lake would have been too quick. I wanted her body to be mutilated. I wanted to hand her back to Crow Barsetti in pieces, so he could look at his only daughter and break down in tears.

The way my mother looked at my father after Pearl Barsetti stabbed him with a knife.

I already knew Vanessa was beautiful because I'd seen her pictures throughout the years. But seeing her in person didn't do those photographs justice. She'd inherited her father's Italian qualities but kept her mother's beauty. As a result, she was gorgeous.

Even I had to admit it.

My arm started to feel numb when we arrived at my villa at the top of the mountain. Blood had seeped into my jacket and my jeans, and if I didn't get it patched up soon, I might have to head to the hospital.

When I kissed her, it was just instinctual. This woman had fought me every step of the way. She had pushed herself to keep going when anyone else would have given up. When she couldn't stand, she crawled. And when she couldn't crawl, she didn't hesitate to tell me to fuck off. I stuck that taser in her neck several times and for a long duration, enough to make her pass out.

But that didn't slow her down.

It annoyed me, but it also impressed me.

I'd never met a person like her.

The odds were stacked against her, but she never showed fear. She never bowed underneath the weight of the situation. Proud and strong, she kept her head held high. When she didn't get away, she tried to crash us off the road. When I walked to the lake, she tried to hot-wire the car. When my back was turned, she found my gun under the seat.

And she shot me.

She fucking shot me.

There was no hesitation before she pulled that trigger. She aimed at my heart, intending to kill me and leave me out there in the snow.

Fuck, it made me so hard.

It turned me on to see a woman submit, to see a woman beg for her freedom. But it was nothing compared to watching a woman fight like that. I'd never seen a woman stand so tall and straight. I'd never seen a woman do anything to survive. She didn't tell me I wasn't a monster or try to convince me to let her go. She didn't try to humanize herself. She knew exactly what I was and didn't sugarcoat it.

I was forced to respect her.

I pulled the van into the garage of my villa, right beside my other cars and trucks, and then we went inside. The house was warm, and the fire was roaring in the hearth. The red carpet took the dirt and snow off my feet, but Richard would clean it up once I went to bed.

Vanessa stopped and looked around, studying her surroundings as she searched for a weapon.

I expected nothing less.

I grabbed the first aid kit tucked in a bookshelf and then sat on one of the couches in front of the fire.

She kept looking around.

"Sit." I opened the box and pulled out the stitching equipment.

She stood in front of the couch, her arms crossed over her chest. The light from the flames made her eyes stand out like jewels.

I pulled out the thread and the needle. "Trust me, you don't want me to ask again." I pulled off my leather jacket, which was now caked with my blood. I pulled my long-sleeved T-shirt over my head next and set it on the coffee table.

Her eyes moved up my body, examining my plethora of tattoos and muscles. Blood was covering most of the ink on my left hand. I had an artist draw out all the bones in my arm and my hand, showing an x-ray with ink. It was a sleeve of tattoos that represented me in the clearest way possible.

"Why should I listen to you?"

"Because I'll stick your hand in the fire just to watch you scream." I looked up at her, telling her not to call my bluff.

She made the right decision and sat down. "I know how to thread, but I've never done stitches before."

"I'll guide you." I grabbed the tweezers, dug them into my flesh, and then pulled out the bullet. I tossed it on the coffee table where guests drank their brandy. Then I covered the wound with a thick gauze, immune to the pain because I'd been shot so many times. My ink made the bullet holes difficult to see, but the women I bedded loved to touch them with their fingertips while I fucked them against my head-board. Once enough pressure had been applied to slow the bleeding, I poured a bottle of vodka over it then told her to start stitching.

She listened to me and got the job done.

Then I wrapped it in gauze and secured it in place.

She set her instruments on the table, which were

caked with blood. "I despise myself for what I just did."

"Third-degree burns are brutal. You'd be crying on the floor right now."

Richard, my caretaker, stepped into the entryway sitting room. He was an older man that I'd found living on the streets in Milan. He lost his wife to cancer, and his only son died in a car wreck. He had been laid off from his job and never got back on his feet. Without having any will to live, he settled for the frozen streets of Milan. So, I offered him a job working for me. "Sir, is everything—" He stopped talking when he spotted Vanessa.

I'd told Richard to stop calling me sir, but he never listened to me. Sir was a bullshit title for an egotistical jackass. I was a murderer and didn't deserve to be addressed so properly. I made my living without honor, and I didn't want to pretend there was anything honorable about me. "Richard, remove all the guns stowed in the house and lock them up in the vault. Turn off the Wi-Fi and shut off cellular service. My guest is a fighter."

"Of course, sir." Richard took the instruction without thinking twice about it. "Anything else?"

"I'm starving. Make dinner."

"Right away." He walked off and left us alone in the entryway.

I grabbed a bottle of scotch and poured myself a drink. I downed it in a single gulp, wanting the liquid to burn a fire in my belly. I refilled my glass.

Vanessa watched my movements. "You're being rude."

"Really?" I asked without interest. "Did this rudeness just start now? Because I've been a dick since the moment we met. Unless your standards are changing in real time."

Her green eyes burned with irritation. "If you're going to kill me, can I at least have a drink?"

"You want scotch? Not some fancy Barsetti wine?"

She snatched the bottle and drank straight out of it. She took a long drink before she set it down, a few drops collecting on her lips. "Now what?"

"What? You want me to kill you right this second?"

"What are you waiting for?" she countered.

"I've got to do it the right way. I want it to sink into your father's brain and never disappear."

Her eyes narrowed with unbridled hostility. "What did my family do to you?"

If only she understood how beautiful she looked when she was angry. It was a shame I'd have to kill her and drop off her body at the Barsetti doorstep. She was paying for the sins of her parents, but the same thing had happened to me. "They ruined my life."

"How so?"

"They killed my father. My mother was left with nothing because his enemies took everything. She turned to prostitution to take care of us. And then a client murdered her and left her body in a dumpster. I was ten at the time."

Despite the unfair circumstances she was in, Vanessa's eyes actually softened into a pitiful look.

"Don't worry," I said. "I killed the guy. Left his body in a dumpster."

"I'm sorry about your mother." Vanessa didn't hesitate to talk back or tell me off. She was honest and violent. If she apologized, it was only because she meant it. The fact that she could see past our differences and actually empathize with me made me feel a little guilty for what I was about to do to her.

But that wouldn't change my mind about it.

"But if my parents killed your father, it must have been for a reason."

It was. And it was justified. But it resulted in my life becoming a shit show. "My father took your aunt as a slave and killed her—"

"Bones?" Her eyes were the widest I'd ever seen them. "Your father was Bones?" She seemed to make the connection because she glanced at my sleeve of tattoos.

"Yes."

She took a deep breath, processing the millions of emotions that just ran through her.

I continued the tale. "My father bought your mother from the Underground and kept her as his new slave. Your father stole her and unexpectedly fell in love with her. And then together, they killed my father."

This must have been news to Vanessa because her eyes softened in defeat. A thin film of moisture covered the surface of her eyes, and her lips quivered slightly. "My mama...he did that to her?" It was the first time she'd shown weakness, overwhelming emotion. She covered her face with her hands and closed her eyes, giving in to the emotion and fighting it at the same time. Her chest heaved as she choked back the sobs. "No..."

I looked away, not wanting to see this strong woman break down in front of me. "Stop crying." The noise was irritating. I didn't like to listen to the way she breathed, the way she sniffed when her nose started to run. It was the first time she cried in front of me, and it was because of the pain of someone else.

She lowered her hands and closed her eyes harder, like she was willing herself to stop. "I said I was sorry about your mother. How could you not sympathize with mine?"

My answer was simple. "Because I'm a monster. You aren't." I took another drink of my scotch, letting the liquor burn my throat on the way down. "That left me in different orphanages without a penny to my name. I was just another poor kid in the system when I should have inherited billions. My legacy was stripped from me, and I turned into another beggar on the street. I became a man, hardened by my experiences. I've made my own fortune, but I've never forgotten where I came from—and who took away what was rightfully mine."

Vanessa stared at the rug on the floor, her eyes still wet from the tears she just shed. "I'm sorry about what happened to you. But my parents did what they had to do. Let's not pretend your father was a good man. You just admitted he was a rapist. He hurt two women in my family, including my namesake. How could you expect my family to do anything different? I'm not ashamed to say I'm glad your father is dead. The world is a better place without him, and he got what was coming to him."

My eyes shifted to her face, the threat distinct in my expression.

She didn't flinch. "And I'll say it again—I'm glad he's dead."

My palm twitched before I struck her. I backhanded her across the face, hitting her so hard she rolled onto the floor. "Say it again."

She quickly pushed herself to her feet, refusing to stay on the ground to recover. Her face was red from the handprint I left. "I'm glad your piece of shit father is dead. And I hope my parents made him suffer."

I lunged at her throat, grabbing her tightly and squeezing so she couldn't breathe. I wanted to kill her this way, to lift her feet from the ground and watch her suffocate. I wasn't delusional about my roots. My father was a bad man. He treated women like animals, got off on hurting them. But if he were still alive, my life would have been better. "Take it back, and I'll let you live."

She held my gaze, gripping my wrist as she tried to squirm away.

"Take it back."

She dug her nails into my wrist then spit on my face.

I threw her hard on the ground, making her thud against the hardwood.

"Never. I'd rather die." She spit at my face again. "My mother is the best person that I know, and the fact that your father did that to her…" Her eyes welled up with tears. "In life and in death, he's my enemy. You're stupid to expect me to think otherwise. And I would rather die right here than betray my family—even if they aren't here to witness it." She moved to her knees and exposed her neck, tilting her head back. "Slit my throat and kill me. Gut me like a pig. I don't give a damn."

My hand twitched at my side, but for a different reason. I had a serious temper, and I'd choked my victims to death many times. Despite the way she insulted me, I felt an invisible restraint. She commanded my respect once again. Barsetti blood ran through her veins like the Nile river, and it was unmistakable that Crow Barsetti was her father.

A part of me pitied her, for telling her the truth about her mother when she had no idea. Her parents probably shielded her from that truth, knowing it would bring tears to her eyes. No mother wanted her child to know she'd been raped.

I was conflicted. I pitied her, but I also wanted to kill her.

She scooted back and took deep breaths now that my hand wasn't wrapped around her throat anymore. "What is your name?"

"You know my name."

"No, you never told me."

I lifted up my left arm, showing the sleeve of tattoos that depicted the various bones in my limb.

Her eyes narrowed. "Your father is your namesake. My aunt is mine."

"The blood war never ended, Vanessa. It's only beginning."

She moved to her feet, holding herself with pride despite the fact that she was half my size and only possessed a sliver of my strength. "You're a wealthy man now. You've made it on your own after coming from nothing. My father would say that's the true test of a man, to make something out of nothing, to stand on his own two feet. You can move on from this and start over. You can end this war for good and change our fate. Let the past go. I'm willing to do that if you are."

Just a second ago, she was livid and emotional. Now she was pragmatic once again, putting aside her hate and focusing on the future. That was a quality of a leader, of a survivor. Her intelligence was keen and her resilience admirable. "My mother wouldn't be dead right now if my father were alive."

"My aunt wouldn't be dead if your father hadn't killed her."

I stared her down, knowing she had the upper hand in the argument.

"Don't expect me to apologize when my family has been the victim in all of this. We retaliated because we had to. My family has walked away from their previous lives and lived peacefully making wine. Let it go."

"I can't."

She sighed deeply, her eyes narrowing. "You can't win this, Bones. Even if you kill me and satisfy your delusional need for revenge, my father won't stop until you're ripped apart. This is a suicide mission."

My life had no value. I was too fucked up in the head to ever live a normal life. I spent my time with whores and made my living as a hitman. Joy wasn't in my vocabulary. Perhaps if my life had been different, I would have had a better chance. The Barsettis were a close clan, loyal to one another and happy. That made me hate them even more. "I know."

3

Vanessa

BONES GUIDED ME TO A BEDROOM ON THE SECOND floor. "Richard has clothes for you on the bed." He turned the knob and pushed the door open. He turned away, like the conversation had been completed.

I was more confused now than I was before. "I thought you were going to kill me."

He was still shirtless because his shirt and jacket were soaked in his blood. He slowly turned around, a man ripped with muscles and strength. Tattoos covered most of his skin, but the black ink couldn't hide the definition of his abs and the thickness of his pecs. Built like a brick house, he was enormous. The muscles in his arms bulged. The only softness he possessed was his blue eyes. They were far too beautiful to belong to a man so spiteful and cold. I wondered if he inherited them from his mother because his father didn't deserve to have them. "Looking forward to it?"

"Just want to know what's going on." A part of me hoped he would change his mind. I needed him to let me go. I was too young to die, and my parents had suffered enough. They shouldn't have to lose their only daughter.

"It takes time to plan the perfect death." He turned his back on me and walked away, the muscles in his back rippling as he moved. He had a deep arch in his back, and his spine was flanked with muscle on either side.

I expected him to take me against my will, especially after he kissed me against the van. But if he was going to do that, it would have happened by now. I walked into the bedroom and shut the door behind me. The door couldn't lock, so I suspected this was the place his other prisoners stayed. The room was plain, with just a bed, a single nightstand, and one window. There weren't bars on the outside of it, and I knew that was because there was nowhere to run. I'd die in the snow and get lost in the darkness if I tried.

I sat on the bed and pulled my knees to my chest. Now that I was alone without a witness, tears burned in my eyes. I thought about my mother, about the horrible things that had happened to her.

My mama.

Bones had raped her and kept her as a prisoner. She was probably beaten just the way my aunt was. She probably suffered every single day until my father rescued her. He took care of her, and they fell in love. My mother had never said where they met, and their past always seemed to be shrouded in mystery.

Now I understood why.

My heart was broken over the knowledge.

It killed me.

And if I died in this place, it would kill them too.

I had to find a way out.

Bones was a man true to his word, and while his motive for killing me was unfair, I didn't doubt he meant it. He wanted to make me suffer so it would hurt my family. Putting a bullet in my head and ending it quickly was too merciful.

He would make it painful.

Maybe even unbearable.

I thought about that kiss against the van. It didn't make any sense. I shot him, and he kissed me in response. He kissed me like he'd never wanted a woman more. Was that a normal reaction for him? Or was there something about me he found attractive?

The last thing I wanted to do was touch him, but seducing him might be my only way out of this.

He was a handsome man, and I did enjoy that kiss. Fucking him might not be so bad. And if it saved my life, it was worth it. Sex was just sex. If I protected my mind, I would be alright. It was a small price to pay if I made it out of there alive.

And back to my family.

———

I DIDN'T SLEEP all night.

I was too paranoid about what might happen if I closed my eyes. I was in my enemy's house, and I couldn't let my guard down when I was this vulnerable. If he came to kill me in the middle of the night, I had to be ready for it.

If he came to fuck me, I had to be ready for that too.

But nothing happened until morning.

Bones didn't knock before he opened the door. His eyes moved to me on the bed, where I sat against the headboard with my ankles crossed. I was still in the same clothes I wore the day before, and I hadn't showered or washed my face.

He was in dark jeans and a black t-shirt, his bright eyes contrasting against his dark clothes. He took me in and absorbed the situation in the blink of an eye. "You've been awake all night?"

With my arms crossed over my chest, I stared him down. "The door doesn't lock."

"And you think a locked door would stop me?" He crossed his arms over his chest, his head slightly tilted.

"The sound would give me some warning."

"And if I came in here with a knife, you'd fight me off?"

It didn't matter how outnumbered I was. I wouldn't give up. "I'd fight like hell."

Like every other time I amused him, his eyes softened

just a little. "I respect that. If you weren't a Barsetti, I might actually like you."

"Even if you weren't your father's son, I still wouldn't like you."

The corner of his mouth rose in a smile. "You've got quite a mouth on you. I enjoyed kissing it."

I enjoyed it too, and I refused to lie about it. He would see right through it anyway. "I'm surprised you didn't force yourself on me."

He tilted his head a little farther. "Did you want me to force myself on you?"

"No," I snapped. "I'm just surprised. You kissed me, so I assumed that was coming next."

"It was just a kiss, baby. Don't read too much into it." He stepped closer to the bed, his hard jaw free of hair because he shaved that morning. Now he wore a clean look. If I met him at a bar or at school, my eyes would be all over him. If he didn't ask me out within five minutes, I'd march over there and ask him out myself.

I didn't understand my enemy at all. How could I defeat someone I didn't understand? I shot him, and he kissed me in response. None of it made sense. "Why did you kiss me?"

"Why do you care?"

"I shot you. I expected you to punch me, not kiss me."

He inched closer to the bed, his thigh almost touching the mattress. "I thought it was hot. Most women would be too weak to pull the trigger. But you did... without a second of hesitation. You wanted me dead. I could see it in your eyes."

"I still want you dead."

His grin widened, the look making him more handsome. "Right there...I like that."

"You like it when I insult you?"

"I like how proud you are. I guess I have a thing for proud women..."

Now was my chance. I could seduce him, welcome him between my legs. I could sacrifice my body for my freedom. It wasn't like I was virgin. He was just another notch on my belt. No one would judge me for doing what was necessary to survive.

His eyes roamed over my body, down my slender neck

and to my tits. He moved farther down my long legs before his gaze returned to mine. He stared at me for several heartbeats, as if he was waiting for something.

Like he was waiting for me to give him permission.

He was a monster and a murderer. His father was a rapist, so he was probably a rapist too. I knew he wanted me, knew he wanted to fuck me then and there. But he remained still, not crossing the line.

"You won't rape me."

His eyes narrowed slightly, darkening in intensity.

"Why?"

He turned away from the bed and headed to the door. "I'll be back for you in an hour."

My heart started to race. "You're going to do it?"

He turned back to me, his hand on the doorknob. "I told you I would, Vanessa. It doesn't matter how much I respect you. It doesn't matter how attracted I am to you. This is bigger than both of us. I will kill you—and I will enjoy it."

———

THE DOOR OPENED AN HOUR LATER. He stood in the same clothes, his expression dark.

I stayed on the bed, too scared to move.

"We can do this the easy way or the hard way."

I swallowed the lump in my throat, feeling my hands shake in terror. The hour of my doom had struck. There was nothing I could do to avoid this. I wished my family were coming to save me like last time, but they had no idea I was missing.

My mother would never recover from this.

My death would make my father cry.

Now I wanted to beg for my life, not so I could keep living, but so they didn't have to suffer.

"How are you going to do it?"

He stayed in the doorway, staring me down with the same indifference. "It's better if you don't know."

I pulled my knees to my chest, my stomach tight. My breathing increased, and now I struggled to remain brave.

He walked to the bed, his powerful arms swinging by his sides. Twice my size and exuding power, he was an opponent I couldn't run from. I couldn't outsmart him either. I tried to defeat him so many times, but it never worked. He leaned down and scooped his arms underneath me before he lifted me.

I let him take me.

He carried me out of the bedroom, treating me like a feather. One arm was underneath my knees while the other supported my shoulders.

I wrapped my arms around his neck and buried my face in his shoulder, not wanting to see where we were going. I clung to him like a woman clung to her lover, finding comfort in my killer's arms.

It was so fucked up.

He carried me downstairs and into a room that was covered with blue plastic. A camera was set up in the corner, and there was a body bag to the side where he would put my corpse once he was done.

I started to shake harder.

He set me on the ground then pulled my shirt over my head.

I didn't fight it, no longer caring.

He undid my bra and stared at my tits once the bra

was gone. He paused to look at me, to stare at my olive skin. He examined my neck, my collarbone, and then dragged his eyes down my stomach to the top of my jeans. He popped the button then pulled down the zipper. He moved to his knees as he peeled away my clothes, pulling my jeans down my legs until I was just in my panties.

He grabbed my hips and rested his face against my stomach, desire oozing from his pores. He kissed the bottom of my belly and then peeled my thong away before he pulled it down my legs. He kissed my thighs until my panties were at my ankles.

This was how I was going to die.

Naked. Alone. Afraid.

I deserved better.

He kept my panties and stuffed them into his pocket, obviously to use later.

When I was dead.

"On your knees." He rose to his full height, turning dark and sinister. The affection he just showed me was long gone.

I stayed upright in defiance.

His eyes narrowed. "Don't make me ask you again."

I slowly moved to my knees.

He came behind me then locked my wrists together with cable ties.

Now I was bound and helpless, naked on a large plastic sheet, so my blood wouldn't damage his beautiful house.

He walked past me toward the camera.

I didn't want to die weak. I wanted to keep my head held high, to pass from this life with respect and dignity. But I wanted to try one more thing. "Take me. I know you want me, Bones. Take me and keep me."

He stopped at the camera but didn't turn around.

It was a long shot. But he just kissed my legs and my tummy, and that wasn't something he would do with any victim. He may be a killer, but he was also a man. He had urges, and if he kept my panties, that meant he wanted me.

He wanted me in the flesh.

"That would only buy you a night. You strike me as a

woman who would rather die untouched than sell her body to live a little longer."

When it came to survival, I was willing to do anything. "When you have me, once won't be enough. You'll want me more and more…and you'll never stop wanting me." It wasn't a reflection of my capabilities in bed. I was just desperate to save my life. I would say anything to make this stop.

He stood still, like he was thinking about what I said.

And then he turned on the camera.

No.

He opened a suitcase and pulled out a long knife.

Oh god.

This was happening.

It wasn't some horrible nightmare.

This was real. I was about to be murdered, and there was nothing I could do to stop it.

The only thing in my control was me.

I refused to go out crying. I refused to beg. I would remain the strong woman that I'd always been. I took a deep breath and controlled my expression, doing my best to seem unafraid. My parents would watch this. I wanted them to be proud of my bravery, even if I was naked and helpless.

Bones walked behind me, holding the blade at his side. He grabbed a fistful of hair and jerked my head back to expose my neck. Then he pressed the blade right against my skin. "Anything you want to say to your family?"

My pulse was strong in my neck. I could feel it vibrate with my panic. This was the last thing I would ever say in this life. I wanted to make it count. "Mama, Father...I know you're going to want to avenge me and hunt down this man for what he did. But please don't. Let this war die with me. Live out your lives in peace and honor my memory over a glass of wine in the evenings. I fought him the whole way, and even now, as he takes my life, he doesn't have me. Please do nothing. The last thing I want is for any more Barsettis to die because of this war. He wants you to come for him. Don't give him what he wants. Please. I love all of you. Goodbye." I closed my eyes and waited for him to slit my throat. I didn't want to know when it was coming.

But it never came. The blade remained against my neck but didn't dig deeper.

I continued to wait.

His hand started to shake.

I opened my eyes, looking at the red light on the camera. I wasn't sure if I felt his hesitation or if he was just enjoying this surge of power.

"Fuck." He pulled his hand away, taking the knife with it. He cut my cable ties then walked to the camera. Instead of turning it off, he smashed it to the ground then stabbed it with the knife. In a violent rampage, he destroyed everything around him.

I was too surprised by what happened to cover myself. I watched him smash apart the camera, stabbing it over and over with the knife. I watched his anger destroy everything in his path. His biceps bulged with rage, and his corded neck became more strained than usual. He finally threw the knife across the room, planting it five inches deep into the wall.

Then he turned around and stared at me.

Furiously.

The vein in his forehead was pounding.

The vein in his neck was throbbing too.

All his muscles flexed and loosened over and over. A

full minute passed as this stare down continued. He dropped the knife, but now it seemed like he was going to murder me with his fists.

I didn't know if I should be relieved or afraid.

Then he rushed me, just the way he rushed me after I shot him. He moved me to my back on the plastic then dug his hand into my hair. His lips crushed against mine, and he kissed me harder than last time.

I kissed him back, my naked body underneath his. I didn't know what was going on, but now that the knife wasn't pressed to my throat, I was high on survival. I wouldn't die today. Maybe he would kill me later, but for right now, I was safe.

So, I kissed him back. I was grateful when I shouldn't be. I felt safe when he was the one who put me in danger. I didn't know what changed his mind, but now that he smothered me with kisses, it didn't matter.

I pulled his shirt over his head, revealing his ripped physique. If the only reason he didn't kill me was because he wanted me, I would let him have me. It'd give me enough time to figure out my next move.

Then my thoughts faded away as he kissed me

harder, giving me his tongue. He breathed into my mouth and moaned directly into my lungs. His hand dug into my hair, fisting it as he gathered more hair into his grasp.

My hands explored his body, feeling the slabs of concrete all over his physique. His pecs were thick like rocks, and his stomach was marked with grooves between his eight pack. His skin was hot like fire, and my fingertips burned as I touched him. My hands moved to his back next, and I felt all the muscles I'd already stared at.

He was so powerful.

The most powerful man I'd ever touched. I felt like I was touching a beast that couldn't be tamed. He was all man, from head to toe. I'd never been with a man who felt so purely masculine. He even kissed me better than any man ever had. Nothing about this was romantic. It was carnal and instinctual, but it frothed with distinct passion.

How could I enjoy kissing someone I hated?

I moved for his jeans next, ready to tug them down so he could fuck me. My offer of sex must have changed his mind. Something about my words got under his skin, made him rethink what he was losing.

I didn't regret the offer I made. I was still alive, and right now, that was all that mattered.

But when I moved for his jeans, he ended the kiss. He moved off me abruptly, like our kiss made him even angrier than he was a moment ago. Huffing and puffing, he got off me then stormed away, leaving his shirt behind.

I lay on the plastic covering, naked and smelling like him. I stared at the ceiling, feeling my hard nipples slowly flatten. Perspiration marked my body because so much adrenaline had circulated through my body. I almost died five minutes ago.

The only reason I was still alive was because Bones changed his mind.

I just hoped he didn't change his mind back.

4

Bones

I SAT BEHIND MY DESK, STILL SHIRTLESS BECAUSE MY temperature had never decreased after I hit my boiling point. I was full of rage, full of ferocity. I stared out the large window to the mountain beyond, looking at the untouched white snow. In the winter, the outskirts of Lake Garda were breathtaking and beautiful. The solitude kept me calm, stopped the bad thoughts from descending.

But right now, they couldn't be helped.

Flames licked the wood and made popping sounds. My bottle of scotch was untouched on the desk. I'd already had plenty for the day. The sun was setting because I'd been sitting there for hours.

And hours.

Her panties were still in my pocket because I intended to jerk off with them after I got rid of her body.

Because I was a sick fuck like that.

My fingers rested against my temples, and I stared out the window, watching the light fade and no longer reflect the powder of snow.

I had the knife at her throat. I had the blade right against her skin. I could feel her frantic pulse as her heart pumped adrenaline in her veins. I got off on her vulnerability, on her submission. She knew her life was about to end, and there was nothing she could do about it. My revenge was finally in my hands.

But then her little speech turned me cold.

She took all the power away—and she didn't even realize it.

She viewed her death as a sacrifice, a way to satisfy my need for revenge and to spare her family at the same time. Like a martyr, she wanted her death to mean something—to be the final end to the war that had existed for three generations.

Once again, she made me respect her. I respected her

selfless view. I respected her strength. I respected the way she didn't cry in her last moment or shit her pants. She held on to her dignity even when she was buck naked.

Not just any woman could manage that.

I wanted to kill her because she was a Barsetti.

But I actually liked this woman.

How did you kill someone you liked?

Fuck. Me.

I stayed in my office for a long time, refusing Richard as he tried to serve me lunch and dinner.

I didn't have an appetite.

Now I didn't know what to do. If I wasn't going to kill her, then what? Just let her go? That'd make me look like the biggest pussy on the planet. I'd lose all my self-respect. And she would tell her family what I did, so they would come after me. Not only would I lose my revenge, but I would also lose my life.

Fuck, this was bad.

———

"SIR?" Richard stepped into my bedroom.

I just got out of the shower, a towel wrapped around my waist. I slept terribly the night before, thinking about her panties in my drawer. I kept wishing I'd killed her, and that led to self-loathing. So I tossed and turned all night. "Call me Bones, Richard."

"You've been telling me that for a long time, but it doesn't feel right."

"Well, it doesn't feel right listening to you address me like that."

He stood with his hands held together in front of his waist, dressed in jeans and a collared shirt. He was the caretaker of the house, managing it when I was gone, but I didn't consider him to be a butler, so there was no reason for him to wear a tuxedo.

"Yes?" I turned back to him, trying to read his silence.

"Your guest is asking for you."

I'd been avoiding her because I knew what she would ask. But I couldn't avoid her forever, and real men shouldn't have to avoid anything. "Is she outside?"

He nodded.

"Send her in."

"Alright." He walked out and shut the door behind him.

Vanessa appeared a moment later, wearing a new pair of jeans and a t-shirt that Richard had supplied for her. It didn't fit because the clothes were a few sizes too big, but this woman could wear a damn poncho and still be model material. Without makeup or doing her hair, she had natural beauty that always made her gorgeous. Something about her high cheek-bones and beautiful eyes made me hard under the towel.

I stared her down, the fire reflecting in her emerald eyes, making them smolder even more. I watched her look me straight in the eye, like she was doing every-thing she could not to stare at my nearly naked body. She'd already seen me shirtless, so I didn't see why it mattered. "I can come back at a different time…"

"Say whatever you came here to say. Don't waste my time."

"Okay…" She cleared her throat, concentrating on my eyes. "I just—"

I dropped the towel in front of her, not caring if she

looked at my dick. Even when I was soft, I was impressive. But when I was hard, I was a behemoth.

"Uh…wow…okay."

I turned to my dresser and pulled out a pair of black boxers, a wide grin on my face. I pulled them up to my waist then turned back to her. "I've seen you naked. Now you've seen me."

Her cheeks were slightly red, despite her olive skin. It was the first time she appeared somewhat flustered. Even when I threw her on the floor and threatened to kill her, she didn't lose her cool. But looking at my fat cock made her shy.

It was cute.

I stood in front of her in just my black boxers. "Yes?"

She crossed her arms over her chest, pressing her tits tightly together. "Are you going to finish getting dressed?"

"I am dressed." Some people thought a suit or armor was the most intimidating clothes to wear, but I disagreed. A strong naked man was far more intimidating. I didn't need a bulletproof vest for protection. The muscle all over my body was all the protection I needed.

Vanessa lost her voice again, obviously uncomfortable by my nudity. She did her best to cover it up, but I was starting to read her better.

"Did you sleep well?"

"Yeah." Her voice was strong again, like she was relieved at the change of subject. She saw my hard dick, and if I was hard, it was because she was in the room. My bulge was still in the front of my boxers, and the more flustered she became, the thicker my girth became. "I hadn't slept in over forty-eight hours, so I couldn't stay awake even if I wanted to."

I'd slept like shit. But the night before, when I'd intended to kill her, I slept like a baby.

"So...what's going on?" she asked bluntly. "Are you going to let me go?"

That wasn't an option. "No."

"Then what?" she pressed. "It won't take long for my family to realize I'm missing."

"They haven't called you yet." I'd been keeping an eye on her phone. Once her parents called and she didn't answer, I'd have to prepare for the worst.

"I never go longer than a week without talking to

my mama."

I loved the way she called her mother that, with deep affection. I hated the Barsettis, but I admired her loyalty to them. Even under threat of torture, she refused to betray them. She didn't want them to be killed trying to avenge her death because she cared more about their safety than her honor. She was a strong and fearless woman, taught to fight with everything she had. She didn't sit around and wait for someone to rescue her. "We'll cross that bridge when we come to it."

"If you're going to keep me, then what are you going to do with me?"

She offered herself to me, offered to bed me until I was satisfied with her. But she warned me that one night together wouldn't be enough. I would just want more of her. That kind of promise aroused me, hearing a woman speak of her bedroom skills with such certainty. I could take her up on that offer, but she only extended it to save her life.

That wasn't why I didn't kill her.

I refused to give an answer. I'd never had a long-term prisoner before. People were dead within the first twenty hours of my captivity. There were dozens of bodies weighed down to the bottom of Lake Garda—all because I put them there.

Vanessa picked up on my silence. "Why didn't you kill me?"

"Who said I still won't?"

She stiffened slightly, but her gaze hardened in response. "If you didn't do it then, you aren't going to."

The corner of my mouth rose in a smile. I loved the way she challenged me, the way she spoke her mind. "I've never thought you were a stupid woman. Don't start being stupid now."

"Then why didn't you kill me?"

I stepped toward her, intimidating her with my size. I moved closer until I was standing over her, the backs of my fingers reaching up to touch her cheek. She didn't have any perfume, so I smelled her natural scent, the smell of the shampoo that was in her bathroom. My fingers brushed against her soft skin, remembering the way I backhanded her so hard. My cock twitched in my boxers. "I didn't kill you. But that doesn't mean I'll ever let you go."

Her eyes slowly narrowed on my face. "Excuse me?"

"You heard what I said."

"You can't keep me here forever. My family will find me."

"You don't have to be in my captivity to be mine, Vanessa."

Her eyes narrowed further, analyzing my words in that smart little brain of hers. "What's that supposed to mean?"

"You'll find out soon enough." I grabbed the waist-band of my boxers and pulled them down, revealing the ten inches of my length. I was fat in all the right places and long the way women liked. I could make a woman come so easily because I could feel her so inti-mately. My dick stretched them wide apart, firing off their nerves in pleasurable ways. My dick could go deep, could hit them in the sweet spot with every thrust. I knew Vanessa was attracted to me. Under threat of death, she kissed me as hard as I kissed her against the van. Then I kissed her again after I spared her life. She was the kind of woman who fought against the overwhelming odds, but when it came to my kiss, she had no fight in her at all.

And now she stared at my dick.

She guessed right when she said I wouldn't rape her. My father had done something terrible to her aunt and her mother. There was no way I could pretend his actions were acceptable. And out of respect for that, I wouldn't do it to her. It was the only way I could make amends for what my father did.

But that didn't mean I didn't want revenge.

She stared at my cock for nearly thirty seconds before she looked at me again. "You want me to fuck you?"

"It's the least you could do since I spared your life."

"You just said you might kill me later," she countered.

I tried not to smile at her wit. "Give me a reason not to."

She held my gaze, absolutely still. She wasn't even breathing.

I waited for her to make her decision, to either walk off or stay. She had every right to say no. She could tell me off and walk back to her room without any repercussions. Or she could let me have her, make me feel better about the stupid decision I made to let her live.

"If I fuck you, you have to let me go."

I considered what she said, disappointed in myself for negotiating with someone who had no power. But my dick was getting harder when I was so close to fucking her. I wanted to pound her into my bed, show her how a real man fucked a woman. "I'll let you leave the house." I chose my words wisely.

"Promise?"

"Men like me don't make promises."

"But when they do, they honor them."

My dick twitched, loving every word that came out of that pretty mouth. "I promise."

Finally satisfied, she stepped closer to me. "Then you have a deal."

The instant I had her permission, my arm slid around her waist, falling against the steep curve in her lower back. Her t-shirt was tight, so I could feel the structure of her body. I'd already studied her frame with my eyes, but to feel my hand glide against her petite body was a new experience. My cock pressed against her stomach, long and enormous. Instead of kissing her, I pressed my lips to her ear. I could feel her breath against me, feel her turn flustered the second the deal was made. I grabbed the back of her neck and kept my lips planted in place, feeling the vein in her neck throb out of control. "Here's another promise, baby." My lips brushed against the shell of her ear as I spoke. "I'll make you come like a man has never made you come before." My father killed her aunt and raped her mother, and the two of us were mortal enemies. But when it came to the carnal chemistry between us, that didn't matter. The heat was there. I could feel it burning just like the flames in my hearth.

She took a deep breath in reaction.

I stepped back but kept my hand on her neck. Then I gently pushed her down, guiding her to her knees on the rug in front of the fire.

She resisted me, choosing to remain upright.

"Baby, you're going to want him to be nice and wet before you take him." I imagined her pussy was just as petite as the rest of her. She would be tight like a virgin because she'd never fucked a man like me before.

Most women hadn't.

Her resistance waned, and she moved to her knees.

I just got Vanessa Barsetti on her knees.

My cock twitched again, watching this powerful woman bow to me. Hostile and uncooperative, she was stubborn like a mule and proud like a queen. So when she obeyed, it was because she wanted to.

And how could that not make me feel like a king?

Women like her turned boys into men. I was already a man, so what would she make out of me?

An emperor.

I stepped toward her, holding the head of my cock against my stomach so it wouldn't hit her in the face. I wanted her to start at my balls, to massage them with her tongue before she glided her tongue over the vein in my shaft.

She hesitated before she parted her lips and pressed a kiss to my sac.

It was just a simple touch, a small beginning, but it was enough to make me clench my jaw and put my body on edge. The infinite muscles of my torso tightened, and my chest ached from the breath I sucked in through my teeth. A sexier woman had never kissed my balls.

She gave her tongue next, swiping it around my textured skin. Her saliva collected on the surface then slowly dripped to the rug underneath us. Then she sucked a ball into her mouth, holding it in place while her tongue massaged it.

Fuck, she was good.

Sucking noises filled the room and added to the sound of the crackling fire. She focused on my balls for a few more minutes, as if she was taking her time before she had to fit my fat dick in her mouth.

I had all night.

And if she struggled to get my dick in her mouth, she'd definitely struggle to get my cock in her cunt.

She finally dragged her tongue up my length, rising on her knees as she moved. Her hand went to my thighs, and she gripped me for balance as she moved farther up. When she reached the head, a drop of pre-come had already formed. She swiped her tongue across it, collecting the juice.

My hand fisted her hair, and I gave a raspy breath.

She lowered herself back to her knees and pulled my cock down, making it parallel to the floor and pointed directly at her mouth. She hesitated before she took it, aware that my size would be an issue.

Which meant she'd never seen a bigger dick in her life.

I tried not to grin at the thought.

She wrapped her fingers around my base and then opened her mouth.

Fuck yes.

She flattened her tongue and pushed her throat over my crown, getting the first few inches inside. She nearly had to unhinge her jaw to keep going, to take in a few more inches until she couldn't go any farther.

"Just a little more, baby." I tugged on the back of her neck, bringing her close to me.

She opened her mouth a little wider and moved, pushing me in the back of her throat before she reached her limit.

"Just like that." I started to guide her forward and back, taking it slow because I was in no hurry to finish. Right now, I just needed her spit to coat my length, so I wouldn't have to break out the lube. Judging by the way she sucked cock so well, she was experienced. But that might not be enough for her to conquer my size.

I'd have to break her in.

She moved forward and back, pushing her throat over my length as far as she could go before she pulled back and took a breath. She did it again, moving slowly and dripping saliva all over my dick and onto the floor.

She kept her gaze focused on what she was doing, and her nails slightly dug into my thighs as she kept working. She did a great job protecting my dick from her teeth, using her tongue as a buffer. Sometimes she had to take a break and pull my cock out of her mouth so she could catch her breath. Her hand jerked me off during those times, smearing her saliva down to my balls.

I only allowed the breaks because she gave such great head in between.

She shoved my dick in her mouth and got back to work, her hands jerking off the bottom part of my dick since she couldn't reach it with her mouth. Her performance wasn't half-assed, and I started to suspect she actually enjoyed herself.

Enjoying my fat cock in her mouth.

I pulled my dick out of her mouth when my balls

started to tighten against my body. "Get on your back."

She wiped the spit from her lips with the back of her forearm and then rose to her feet. She stripped off her clothes, pulling her shirt over her head then unclasping her bra. I'd already seen her naked, so this sight shouldn't impress me, but once her jeans and panties were off, my cock became a little happier.

I wanted to jerk off and stare at her.

She lay on my bed, her head against the pillow and her knees together.

I pushed my boxers to my ankles and kicked them away before I climbed on the bed and moved on top of her. The mattress sank under my weight, making Vanessa dip slightly underneath me. With a flat tummy, small and perky tits, and the most beautiful skin, she was exceptional.

I could honesty say a more beautiful woman had never been in my bed.

I had fantasies about securing her hands to the head-board, of having my way with her against her will. I was a monster, and that would never change. But finding her underneath me out of choice was even better.

My arms slid behind her knees and positioned her wide apart, making her as open as possible. It would take a few minutes to get my cock inside her, even when it was soaked with her saliva. I held myself above her and pressed my cock right against her clit and started to grind.

She tensed at the contact, her nipples hardening and her eyes closing for a brief moment. She took a deep breath, her chest tinting with a beautiful red color on her dark skin.

I moved my face above hers and watched her reaction to me, watched her body enjoy the hard stimulation my cock was giving to her clit. I stared at her lips, looking at the curve of her bow, and then I kissed her.

It was slow, unlike all the other times I kissed her. I wanted to take my time, to get her as wet as possible so my cock could bury itself inside her. I sucked her bottom lip gently before I gave her my tongue.

She kissed me back, her hands remaining by her sides.

I breathed into her, moving slightly faster and deeper.

Kissing a woman was the last thing on my mind. When I picked up women, I wanted them to suck my cock instead of kiss me on the mouth. Kissing was for young people or people in love.

But I loved kissing Vanessa.

It was so damn good.

Her hands eventually moved to my arms, feeling the sections that divided the different groups of muscles. Her fingertips explored my shoulders and my chest, and I knew she loved my body. She stared at it enough times to give herself away.

She kissed me back with the same passion she showed before, falling into a rhythm with me. Every time my cock pressed against her clit just right, her nails slightly dug into me. Soon, it didn't feel like a deal had been struck between us. She wasn't bartering for her freedom. We were just a man and a woman who wanted each other to get off.

I couldn't wait to feel that pussy, to take Vanessa Barsetti and make her mine. I couldn't even imagine how amazing her cunt would be. And I'd pump so much of my come inside—pile after pile.

I couldn't wait any longer. Her kiss was only turning

me on more, and my cock was about to explode. I pushed down on my shaft and pointed my crown at her entrance, feeling the moisture greet me.

She wanted me bad.

I pushed inside her slightly, feeling her arousal surround me.

I couldn't help but smile as I kissed her. "Baby, you want this cock as much as I want to give it to you." I broke our kiss and stared into her eyes, seeing the unmistakable look of arousal. She wanted my fat cock even though it would hurt. She wanted me buried deep inside her, not just so she could be free. There was no mistaking her hatred. She despised me as much as she did before. But her dislike couldn't interrupt her needs.

I started to sink farther.

"Stop." She pushed against my stomach, stopping me from going any deeper. "Put on a condom."

I wasn't putting on a damn thing. I was coming deep inside her. Vanessa Barsetti was going to be overstuffed with my come by the end of the night. "I know you're on birth control."

She was still aroused, her legs spread to me, but

annoyance crept into her expression. "And how do you know that?"

I glanced at her arm, where there was still evidence of the shot she'd received. I was observant of everything around me, to the minor details no one else paid attention to.

"That's not what I'm worried about."

"I'm clean."

"And I'm just supposed to believe you?" she asked incredulously. "You killed a man in an alleyway, and you've taken me as a hostage. You expect me to believe you?"

"Have I ever lied to you?" I challenged.

She shut her mouth.

"I always wear a rubber when I fuck a woman. But with you, I'm giving you all my come. And trust me, you're going to want it. Every woman should feel her man's come deep inside her."

"You aren't my man."

I forced myself a few inches inside her, making her suck in a breath through her teeth. I felt her moisture surround me further, felt her walls constrict around me. "Right now, I am." I pushed a little harder, fighting her body's tightness as I crept farther inside. I was wet and she was wet, but our size differences were a serious obstacle.

She stopped fighting me, her nails digging into my arms and her breathing escalating. She stared into my eyes as the fire danced in her gaze. She breathed harder as she took more of me, her tiny cunt doing its best to take my dick.

I kept sinking until I couldn't go any farther. She took most of my length, but I reached a dead end when I hit her cervix. I closed my eyes and savored the feeling of her phenomenal pussy. So wet, so tight. I loved all pussy, but hers was truly exceptional. I wanted to stay buried in there forever. I could come right now if I wanted to.

But I had to fulfill my promise.

I opened my eyes and stared into hers as I started to thrust, making sure my body ground against her clit with my movements. I sank deep inside her and pulled out again, my headboard creaking with my motion.

She breathed through my thrusts, struggling to take my cock. "Fuck...you have a big dick."

I shoved myself completely inside her just to validate her statement even more. "I know. It's all yours." As much as I wanted to fuck her aggressively, I gave it to her slow. She was getting used to my size, and I was enjoying her performance. I watched her eyes well up with tears as she fucked me through the discomfort.

It fucking turned me on.

Her hands moved to my shoulders, and she used them as an anchor, her nails clawing into me. She bit her bottom lip and breathed through her nose.

Minutes later, her cunt finally started to loosen. We moved together easier, and I was sheathed in her cream as she started to really enjoy it. I fucked her a little harder, sank a little deeper.

She dragged her hands down my chest, biting her bottom lip over and over again. A concentrated expression came over her face, and she started to sweat even though I was doing all the work.

I knew what was coming.

"Baby." I kissed her, giving a slight tug on her bottom lip. "Come for me."

She resisted me, wanting me to break my promise. "No."

I fucked her harder, pounding her into the mattress and giving her so much of my dick that she couldn't fight it for long.

Moans escaped her lips and her nails dug deeper into my flesh, nearly drawing blood. Her pussy became so wet, and just as it was in the beginning, it started to tighten up. But this time, it was for a different reason. "No…"

A shiver ran down my spine when I felt her body betray her. I took control, pressed her buttons and made her do exactly what I wanted. My cock was calling all the shots, and it conquered her pussy. "Don't fight it. Enjoy it." I worked up a sweat as I fucked, my ass tightening over and over as I gave it to her good.

She finally let go, her body writhing as her moans turned to screams. She grabbed on to me so she had something to hold, and the face she made when that climax hit her…was unbelievable.

Fuck.

I watched her face turn red, watched her mouth open with her screams. I watched her green eyes light up like fireworks. Her screams filled my bedroom, and her pussy gripped me with a force that defied her size.

"God…" Her head rolled back, and she writhed, her hips still bucking and her nipples sharp like the tip of a diamond.

Fuck, I couldn't keep going. Not after that.

I gave my final thrusts before I joined her, giving her all my come deep inside that tight little cunt. My biceps and triceps clenched tightly as I held my body on top of her and felt the rush explode through me. My cock twitched as I released, the mounds pouring deep inside her. It was a climax I wouldn't forget, an orgasm that was more intense than usual.

I stayed inside her until every drop was deep within her. My cock had thickened to its fullest point, and then it started to soften once more. It was the greatest satisfaction I'd ever known. I'd never gotten off quite like that, and I'd whipped a woman until she bled all over the floor.

Once the wave of pleasure disappeared, the red tint in her face slowly started to fade away. Her green eyes still sparkled, but soon, shame crept into her features. She could downplay the climax she just had.

But we both knew the truth.

I slowly pulled my cock out of her, feeling the tightness of her pussy when I wasn't at full mast. I turned over and lay beside her, my sweaty back hitting the sheets. I tucked one arm behind my head and caught my breath, more satisfied than I'd ever been in my life.

She stayed beside me and pulled the sheets to her chest, hiding her tits from view.

It didn't matter if she covered herself, her naked body was permanently ingrained in my mind.

I closed my eyes and listened to the sounds of the fireplace as the flames started to trickle down until they were just simmering coals. I didn't usually sleep with my ladies, especially when it was handled as a transaction. But I was too comfortable to care if Vanessa slept beside me.

"Do you want me to leave?" she asked, sitting up and keeping the sheet against her chest.

"I don't care."

I felt her body shift as she turned to look at me. "You strike me as the kind of guy to kick out a woman as soon as you're finished."

"You're right. But I'm gonna fuck you first thing in the morning, so you may as well stay here." I didn't open my eyes, not needing to see her face to predict her moods.

"How do you know I won't kill you in the middle of the night?"

A grin formed on my lips. "Give it your best shot, baby."

"You're either very arrogant or stupid. All I have to do is grab a big vase and smash it over your skull."

I finally opened my eyes and looked at her. "You've shot me, and I didn't break my stride. You think a vase is going to do anything? You called me a monster for a reason. I'm not just evil, but enormous. So if you're going to make your move, make sure it counts." I closed my eyes again. "Besides, you won't do a damn thing."

"You just said I shot you."

"But I spared your life. I could have butchered you, but I didn't."

"That doesn't mean I owe you anything."

"You're right," I said. "But you feel like you owe me anyway."

WHEN I WOKE up the next morning, it was bright and early. I didn't usually go to bed so early, but fucking Vanessa knocked me out. I woke up in the exact same position I fell asleep in, my hand tucked under my head.

Vanessa lay beside me, sound asleep and directly at my side. The covers were pulled to her shoulder like she was cold. The fire died a long time ago, and the heater in this house couldn't keep up with the constant freezing temperatures. She probably moved closer to me during the night to stay warm.

Just as I predicted, she didn't try to kill me.

It was far too risky, even if I was unconscious. She thought she would be free soon, so it didn't make sense to gamble that possibility by making a move. Even if she slammed a vase over my head, it wouldn't kill me. But it would piss me off.

And then I might actually kill her.

I rubbed the sleep from my eyes then stared down at her, seeing her slightly parted lips and the way her hair dragged behind her on the pillow. The crisp white sheets made her skin appear darker in comparison. She and I looked nothing alike. My skin was fair like the snow outside, traits I inherited from my American mother. I had crystal-blue eyes like the tropical ocean. My hair was slightly blond, and her hair was nearly black.

She was perfect.

A real man knew how to appreciate a beautiful woman, and the longer I stared at her, the more I wanted to appreciate her. The idea of killing her still got me hard, but I'd much rather fuck her again.

And again.

I hooked her arm around my waist and then rolled her to her back.

She kept her eyes closed and stayed asleep, but she stirred slightly, feeling her body move but not caring what happened.

I was already hard for her, anxious to fill her with more come so it would drip onto my sheets. Maybe I didn't kill this Barsetti but I just fucked her.

That was better in some ways.

I separated her thighs then slid inside her, the head of my cock pushing through her tight entrance.

When she felt the pressure between her legs, her eyes fluttered open. "Jesus, do you mind? I'm sleeping."

I pushed farther inside her, sinking as my shaft stretched her apart. "Then keep sleeping." I moved as far as I could go, feeling the same incredible pussy that I felt last night.

"You would fuck an unconscious woman?" she asked incredulously.

"If it was you, fuck yes." Last night, I took it slow. But this time, I fucked her good and hard. I dug my hips deeply into her, pushing my entire length inside as my pulsing dick explored her just as intimately as last time. My headboard tapped against the wall, and I brought heat into the room with my movements.

Her body shuddered under my pressure, her tits shaking up and down. Her eyes were still lidded with sleep, but she didn't make another protest. Her arms wrapped around my neck, and she buried her face into my shoulder, pulling her legs apart so I could have her.

So I could keep fucking her.

It was a lazy fuck, the perfect kind for first thing in the morning. I thrust and I fucked, driving my big dick inside this beautiful pussy. I didn't care about getting her off, but I wanted to prove I could make her feel good even if she didn't want to.

So I made her come—like a man.

I listened to her scream right against my ear, her nails clawing at my back so hard they almost drew blood.

Then I came inside her, adding more come to the pile I made last night. I dumped all my seed inside her, stuffing her full until it overflowed onto the sheets. I groaned as I finished, loving my conquest.

I caught my breath before I moved off and got out of bed.

She lay there, full of my warm come.

I pulled on jeans and a t-shirt then walked out.

Her voice stopped me at the door. "Where are you going?"

All I did was give her an angry look in response.

———

I SAT in my office with the phone pressed to my ear. I listened to it ring a few times before Max answered.

"Haven't heard from you in a while. Started to worry."

"I thought you said you didn't care whether I lived or died?"

"I don't," he said with a chuckle. "My concern is strictly for my self-interest."

I grinned, knowing he was only being partially truthful.

"He's dead?"

"He's sitting at the bottom of Lake Garda."

"Such a beautiful place. Too good for him, if you ask me."

"Cold as fuck, though."

"I'll talk to my client and wire the funds."

"Good." I made my fortune as a hitman. I executed men for money. It was the simplest job in the world. I had one task and full autonomy to fulfill it however necessary. It paid my bills and gave me a life of luxury. It wasn't close to the billions I should have inherited, but it was enough. "I had an issue."

He turned serious. "What kind of issue?"

"Some woman walked by and witnessed my murder streak. I caught her and was about to slit her throat... but then I recognized her."

"You recognized her?" he asked. "Who was she?"

I still couldn't believe all the events happened coincidentally. The Barsettis were my mortal enemy, and to see the youngest one walk by at the perfect moment was unbelievable. I'd seen Conway Barsetti at the Underground one night when I was in disguise, but he didn't possess the same allure as his younger sister. "Vanessa Barsetti."

"Shit...what did you do?"

"I didn't have any other choice. I took her."

"You killed her, right?"

I never answered.

"Bones, you have to kill her. If she tells her family—"

"I'm aware of the situation."

"And you want to kill her anyway..."

"I did." I still do, a little. "But when it came down to it...it didn't work out."

"That's not like you."

"I know." I was cold and brutal. I didn't think twice before taking a life. Cruelty was in my blood. I lacked empathy and compassion. I was born of a different breed, so unattached to human emotion that I couldn't understand it. "But I've made use of her…"

Max knew exactly what that meant and didn't ask for clarification. "What happens when they know she's missing?"

"I haven't figured that out yet. I was thinking of letting her go…but keeping her under my thumb."

"How would you enforce that?"

I had a few ideas. "I'm not sure yet."

"Whatever you do, don't underestimate her. She's a Barsetti."

The corner of my mouth rose in a smile, thinking of all the badass stunts Vanessa pulled while in my captivity. Against all odds, she still pushed on. When grown men wouldn't get up again, she rose to her feet. She didn't hesitate before she shot me. Her Barsetti blood made her absolutely fascinating. "I know."

5

Vanessa

BONES FUCKED ME THEN DISAPPEARED.

He was gone all day, so I showered and then put on a new pair of clothes that were set out on my bed. The clothes were a little baggy again, but I didn't complain.

I wouldn't be here much longer.

I hadn't had time to think about what was going on between Bones and me. I bartered for my freedom by fucking him, and he vowed to make me come.

I did everything I could to prove him wrong. I didn't want that man to be right. I didn't want to be the victim of a kidnapping and then enjoy my tormentor.

I didn't think it was possible to get wet for a man who held a knife to my throat.

But I wasn't wet—I was soaked.

It was humiliating.

It made me hate him more.

I despised his arrogance. I despised his power. He moved between my legs that morning and helped himself like I was a toy rather than a person. He got right to the point and fucked me harder than he did the night before.

And to make it worse, I came again.

Goddammit.

I tried to make myself feel better by convincing myself I was subjected to my anatomy. If you rubbed anything the right way, magic would happen. But there was no denying I'd never come that hard in my life. I'd never had a bigger man inside me, a man who could stretch me to maximum capacity. Not only did he have the right tools, but he knew how to use them. I'd dated nice guys, even hot guys. There was chemistry and excitement. There was good sex at my apartment.

But nothing compared to that.

Why did the best sex of my life have to happen with my mortal enemy?

With the man my family had a never-ending blood war with?

Why didn't I just take a different route home?

I'd only been there for a few days, so I hadn't explored the house. We were in a mansion on the hillside of a snowy mountain. All the windows showed the breathtaking view of the snow. I couldn't see the lake from up here because we were too high up.

I didn't see an escape route. Even if I could steal one of the cars from the garage, driving in the terrain would be tricky. I hardly drove in the snow, and since I had to drive slowly, I probably wouldn't make it far before he caught up with me.

Richard appeared around the corner, a casual butler that was nothing like Lars, the man who had been serving my family since my father was young. Richard didn't have the same curt mannerisms as Lars, and he was always in jeans. "Vanessa, Bones wants you to join him for dinner."

"Address me as Ms. Barsetti." I wasn't getting any respect around here, and now I needed to demand it.

Richard's expression didn't change at my request. "Alright. Dinner is served. Will you be joining him?"

"Do I have a choice?"

He shrugged. "You could say no, and I'll report that to him. And then he'll tell me to come get you again. If you refuse then, he'll get angry and come after you himself…so you have a choice. But no matter what your choice is, you'll end up in the same place. But perhaps it'll make you feel better because you'll feel like you had a say in the matter…even though you never really did."

The thought was depressing. As long as I was in this house, I was subjected to the desires of this psychopath. I didn't have any rights, and my attitude seemed to turn him on even more.

Because he was a freak.

"So…" Richard brought his hands together at his waist. "How do you want to do this?"

I was hungry, so putting up a fight right now didn't sound that appealing. "What's for dinner?"

"Bones's favorite. Steak, potatoes, and greens."

Damn, that sounded pretty good. "Dessert?"

A small smile crept into his lips. "Blueberry pie and ice cream."

I didn't have to think it over long. "Alright. I'll eat with him." When I lived with my parents, I had the best chef in the world provide all my meals. I always ate like a queen, having culinary feasts I never really appreciated. Now that I lived alone, I ate a lot of peanut butter and jelly sandwiches and chips. I never learned to cook, and it seemed pointless when my skills would never compare to the culinary genius that Lars possessed. I would just hire a chef myself, but I was too broke for that.

I walked into the dining room where the grand table sat. A large window took up the entire wall, and it showed a view of the mountainside. Snow was falling, hitting the piles of fresh powder softly.

Bones sat there, a short glass of scotch in front of him. The bottle beside him was half empty, telling me he already had a few glasses before I arrived. His eyes shifted to me immediately, and he stared at me with the same intensity he always wore.

Like he might kill me.

I sat across from him.

"Wine?" Richard opened a bottle of red. On the label was a brand I recognized. Barsetti Vineyards.

"Thanks for trying to make me feel at home," I said sarcastically. "And yes. I'll take a full glass."

Richard poured it before setting the bottle on the table. "I'll grab the dishes." He walked into the kitchen, leaving us alone together.

Whether Richard was there or not, Bones stared at me the exact same way. He stared like there was nothing he wanted more than to strangle me—and fuck me. His broad shoulder blocked the chair behind him completely, and his tattoos peeked from underneath his shirt to his neck. His fingers were wrapped around his glass, and he brought it to his mouth to take a drink.

I expected him to make a smartass comment or two, but it never happened. He continued to stare, like I was a TV screen or a piece of artwork that he could watch for hours. Direct eye contact didn't make him the least bit uncomfortable.

It didn't make me uncomfortable either. He failed to

intimidate me, so I held his gaze and enjoyed my wine.

If you stripped away the crime and the blood war, he was so beautiful that he was hard to look at. He could walk into any bar and have the attention of every single woman in the room. Not only was he a power-house, but he had unbelievably handsome features. Those blue eyes were hard not to stare at.

It was a shame he chose this life. So much failed potential.

"What are you thinking?" He set his glass down, and his hand continued to rest on the hardwood table. His forearms were chiseled just like the rest of his body, the sections of muscle identified by grooves. His veins streaked across, bulging in comparison.

"What are you thinking?" I countered.

"You really want to know what goes on in this sick fucking mind?" The corner of his mouth rose in a smile, amused like always.

"I've already experienced the worst of it."

He took another drink. "Or the best."

I refused to react, keeping the same stoic features.

He wiped his mouth with the back of his forearm. "I was thinking about how beautiful you look like that... with that jet-black hair and olive skin. You don't have a drop of makeup on, but your features are still phenomenal. You're stunning. So fucking stunning that I'm not sure if I can wait until after dinner to fuck you." He finished the scotch in his glass then set it down with a loud thud. "What were you thinking, baby?"

"Stop calling me that."

"I can call you whatever I want. Now answer the question."

His answer wasn't as sick as he forecasted, and I was annoyed with myself for actually appreciating his response. "I was thinking it's a shame you've decided to live your life this way."

"In what way?" he countered. "I live in a mansion—and I own several more of them. I have a butler. I'm rich. I have—"

"Wealth isn't everything. It'll never buy you happiness." I lived a life of luxury, but when I reflected on the happiest moments of my life, they had nothing to do with money. They were times when I was surrounded by friends and family, enjoying the Tuscan sun with a bottle of wine and a good cheese.

He cocked his head slightly, his eyes narrowing. "Don't interrupt me again."

I wanted to fire back with something rude, but my gut told me to listen to him.

"I'm not ashamed of what I do for a living. I didn't have the resources you did. I didn't go to a private school or have a father to pay for university. My mother was a whore to make sure I had food every night. Is it also a shame that she lived her life that way?"

"I never said that."

"And now I'm asking." Without raising his voice, he increased the tension in the room. He turned hostile without a single movement, becoming silently deadly. "Because I'm not ashamed of her. I'm not ashamed of what she did to provide for me. Like any other mother, she did whatever was necessary to make sure I had clothes, shoes, and supplies so the other kids wouldn't make fun of me." He leaned over the table, his elbows resting on the wood. "You think less of her?"

It didn't matter how much he threatened me. I wouldn't cave. So I answered honestly. "Never."

His intense gaze remained, his blue eyes burning into mine.

"Never underestimate what a mother will do for her child…" My own mother never told me the horrible truth of her past. She did it to protect me, to make sure I wouldn't have to carry the grief that now sat in the pit of my stomach. "But I judge you for killing people in alleyways and capturing a young woman for revenge. I judge you for demanding sex in exchange for my freedom."

"Like you didn't want to fuck me."

My eyes narrowed. "No, I—"

"I made you come in less than two minutes. You enjoyed every fucking second of it. Let's not rewrite history and paint you in a fictional light. I kissed you against my van, and you kissed me back. I kissed you on the floor just seconds after I held a knife to your throat. I fucked you in my bed and listened to you moan for me, felt your nails slice into my skin. I listened to your screams when my fat dick hit you in the right place. I may not be a good man, but you'll always have my honesty. I deserve the same from you."

It was the first time a man shut me up. He didn't tell me to be quiet, but his argument left me speechless. There was no way I could contradict any of those things, not when we both witnessed them. "Whether I wanted to fuck you or not, I want my freedom."

"Freedom is a privilege, not a right."

"Not according to the law."

"In the underworld, there is no law. There are only rules—my rules."

I crossed my arms over my chest, my appetite suppressed now that this conversation took a deadly turn. I refused to give in to the fear, but I couldn't deny how lethal this guy was. He didn't kill me, but he was definitely temperamental. "When are you going to let me go?"

He grabbed the bottle and refilled his glass. "I'll let you leave the house in a few days." He worded it the same way as last time—and that was unsettling.

"My mother will call soon."

"She hasn't yet."

"You're keeping an eye on my phone?"

"Yes."

"Can I have it back?"

He laughed into his glass before he took a drink.

Richard entered the dining room with our entrees. Two steaks with roasted potatoes and asparagus. He set the dishes in front of us, topped off my glass with wine, and then set a basket of bread on the table before he walked out.

Once the succulent food was placed in front of me, my appetite came back. I grabbed my fork and knife and dug in.

Bones watched me for a few seconds before he started eating.

"What am I supposed to do for the next few days?"

"Don't be stupid." He cut into his steak then placed a large piece of meat in his mouth. "I prefer it when you're smart, even when you won't shut your mouth. You know your only job is to lie in whatever position I ask while I fill you with my endless loads." He cut into his steak again and took another bite, like this was an appropriate conversation to have over dinner.

A tiny chill ran down my spine, and that made me despise myself. "I was under the impression this was just a one-night thing."

"You're the one who told me I wouldn't just want you once—but I wouldn't stop wanting you. Looks like you made good on your word." He put another piece of steak into his mouth and chewed, his hard jaw working while his eyes focused on my face.

"And you think that's going to change in a few days?"

He kept chewing, the tension escalating between us. "There's a good chance it won't."

"But you promised you would let me go."

"I promised I would let you leave the house."

"Is that not the same thing?"

He didn't answer. "I told you I would never let you go, whether you're in my captivity or not."

"The second I'm out of here, you'll have no power over me."

"That's what you think. But you've never been in the presence of real power." He spoke with such confidence that I didn't want to challenge him.

I was the daughter of a very powerful man. My uncle had the same influence, and I knew my mother didn't take shit from anybody. But my family had walked away from a life of crime and danger. Their power was enforced by respect, not fear. Bones was different, a type of enemy I didn't know how to combat.

"Eat your dinner. I don't want you to be hungry later." He dropped his gaze for the first time, looking down at his food. His muscles shifted and worked together to accommodate his movements. Even the slightest maneuvers forced his muscles to bulge noticeably. Not only was he a large man, but his muscles were ripped and tight. They were pulled close to his skeletal frame, making him an extremely heavy mass. I would know…since I'd been underneath him.

I picked up my fork and continued eating, knowing what was coming next once dinner was over. If he were any other man, the situation would make me sick to my stomach. But no matter how much I hated him, the truth couldn't be denied.

I was attracted to him.

———

WHEN I STEPPED into his bedroom, I spotted the red rug underneath his bed. His stone fireplace was larger than usual, reaching high off the ground so it could illuminate his entire bedroom. With dark wood furniture and paintings of the landscape around Lake Garda, I felt like I was hidden away in a chalet in Switzerland instead of a few hours outside of Milan.

My eyes moved to the bed, and that was when I spotted the lacy black lingerie.

That was definitely for me.

There was a note, scribbled in his masculine hand-writing. *Put this on, baby.*

My eyes narrowed at the word *baby*, and I crumpled the note in my hand and tossed it on the ground. I picked up the black baby doll with the push up bra and held it up to my body. There was a black thong with it, a G-string that barely covered anything.

He had specific tastes.

I'd never put lingerie on for a man. I'd never been in a serious relationship that garnered the occasion. My life was full of flings, men I hoped would become something more until my interest fizzled out.

I pulled it on then fixed my hair. I wasn't wearing any

makeup because I didn't have any here. It wasn't like I'd packed a bag and took off for the weekend. I examined myself in his vanity, fixing my black hair until it framed my face. Without eye liner and mascara, my eyes didn't pop like they usually did. When I wore red lipstick, it highlighted the bow-curve of my upper lip, and now I wished it were highlighted.

Bones liked me this way, but I wished I looked better.

Not that I should care to look better for him.

He stepped out of the bathroom, his shoulders still slightly wet from the shower he just took. He didn't come out with a towel like last time. He came ready for the occasion.

He stopped and stared at me, his eyes roaming over the lingerie he left for me. He started at my neck then slowly trailed his eyes down my body. He focused on my tits before he admired the curves of my waistline. Farther he went, moving down my legs before he lifted his gaze back to my face.

Like a shark circling his prey, he started to move.

He walked around me, getting closer and casting a shadow across the room. He was a head taller than me, so he dominated me with his size without even standing perfectly straight. He stopped when he was directly in front of me, his face tilted down so he could look at me.

My heart was beating so fast.

I'd already been with him twice, but I was even more nervous than before. My attraction wouldn't change the fact that this man was terrifying. He scared me sometimes, when he looked at me with those predatory eyes. I felt like prey, like there was nothing I could do to escape this brutal man. I was his—and there was nothing I could do about it.

He started at my stomach. He gripped my waist, his hands large enough to completely reach around my tummy, from thumb to finger. His thumbs pressed against my belly button, and he squeezed me gently, showing that he had my life in his hands. He stared down at me, his blue eyes concentrated on my curves.

My hands went to his forearms because I wanted to feel the chiseled muscles of his arms. I wanted to feel his corded veins and the light amount of dark hair. My fingers could wrap around his girth the way he could wrap his hands around my waist.

He moved his forehead to mine, his fingers gently

tugging me closer to him. I felt like a slave, obedient and still. I was his to enjoy, and I had to wait until he found something he wanted to take.

He moved his hands to my chest, his palms right above my tits. My heart was beating so fast and now he could feel it. Now he knew how nervous I was, how much his proximity affected me. I could put on a brave face and pretend to be unafraid of the entire world, but when it came to my heart, it didn't lie.

His right hand moved farther up until he reached my neck. He wrapped his fingers completely around, getting me in the perfect grip if he wanted to choke me. His fingers pressed into me threateningly.

I held my breath. I focused my gaze on his chest, seeing the black ink that was all over his body. Some of the images were of skulls or blades. Some were small trees, and another was a European soldier from the second world war. His body was a canvas, and I wondered what the artwork meant.

His hand loosened toward my jawline, and he swiped his thumb across my bottom lip.

I closed my eyes. Feeling him want me and taking his time made it more intense than before. Last time, he couldn't wait to get inside me. He was desperate to shove his cock in my mouth and in my pussy. But now, he had the restraint to slow down even more.

He pulled his head back and met my gaze head on. "I'm the first man you've ever been with."

My eyes stared into his beautiful blue ones, seeing an evil soul behind that handsome expression. He was too pretty to be so mean, but his heart was painted black. It was mutilated by his suffering, and he would never recover. "No..." I'd been with several guys since I became an adult. Waiting until marriage had never been right for me. I wanted to make sure my husband and I would have good sex for the rest of our lives, so I believed in taking the car for a test-drive before I bought it. My brother and cousins had been with more women than I could even count, so there was no reason I couldn't explore my sexuality too. As a result, I knew exactly what I liked and what I wanted. I was definitely not inexperienced. Bones had an exceptionally big dick, so taking him was like losing my virginity all over again.

His hand slid into the fall of my hair, and he gripped me tightly, adjusting my face to look at him head-on. "They were boys. I'm a man." His eyes shifted to my lips. "You're all woman, from head to toe. I've never laid eyes on a more beautiful woman, so damn sexy and strong. I'll make you forget any other man has ever been between your legs. I'll wipe away their memory and make you think of me when you touch yourself."

"You're awfully cocky…"

He tugged on my hair a little harder. "Because I earned it." His hand released my hair and slid down to my shoulder. His finger hooked in the strap and he pulled it off my shoulder, revealing my bare skin.

He craned his neck down and kissed it, sucking my skin aggressively and even giving it a gentle bite.

I closed my eyes and suppressed the moan that wanted to emerge from my throat. My hands immediately reached out and gripped his torso, feeling my thumbs slip on his abs because they were so smooth.

He kissed up my neck until his lips hovered over my ear. He breathed hard, his arousal audible in the simple sound. His hand pulled down my other strap until my other shoulder was revealed. "Tell me how you want me to fuck you, baby."

My hands gripped his hips, still using him for balance. My breathing matched his, feeling the same arousal in my veins as he felt in his lungs. My thumbs pressed into his, and I kept my eyes closed, overwhelmed by his control over me.

"Tell me, baby."

When I was with a man, I liked to be on top. I liked to go at the pace I wanted, to grind my clit against his pelvic bone as I moved. Watching his face darken with arousal as he watched me just turned me on more. "I want to fuck you…"

The next breath he released was louder than all the others, showing his surprise and his approval. His hands moved to my hips, and he played with the lace of my thong before he stepped away. The muscles of his back tightened and shifted as he walked away, his powerful shoulders sexy in the light of the flames. He moved on the bed and sat against the headboard, his large dick lying against his stomach. He wrapped his hand around his shaft and slowly jerked himself. "Strip." He rested his mass against the wooden head-board, his chest rising and falling with his deep breathing. He was rock-hard and drooling from the tip.

I pulled the baby doll over my head, taking some of my hair with it. I stood in just my panties and walked closer to the bed, my fingers hooking into the straps at my hips.

His eyes followed my hands, staring at the way I played with myself.

I slowly pulled my panties down, taking my time before I finally revealed the nub between my legs. When I stood upright again, he stared right at my most intimate place, squeezing his dick a little harder. When he motioned for me to sit on his lap, all he gave was a slight nod of his head, his jaw hard from the way his teeth were clenched tightly together.

I moved onto his lap, my thighs parted over his hips. He was a big man, so I felt weightless putting my entire body on him. My pussy sat right against his hard cock, and the instant I felt just how thick he was, a jolt of electricity ran through my stomach.

He sat upright against the headboard, his long legs stretched out across the bed. He had muscular thighs and toned calves, every part of his body chiseled to perfection. I'd never seen a more powerful man buck naked. The men I dated were usually fit, but not as intensely as this man.

I felt his cock twitch underneath me.

Because he was that big.

Big enough to move a mountain with that log.

His hands slid up my thighs until he reached my ass. He gripped both of my cheeks and pulled me a little closer, bringing my chest next to his. My nipples hardened when I felt his bare skin, the hardness of his sleek muscles.

My hands moved up his pecs to his shoulders, feeling the part of his body that I enjoyed the most—besides the part I was sitting on. My fingers felt the individual grooves of muscle, and I admired his broadness. I loved the way his size stretched a t-shirt, his hardness too big to be contained in the cotton.

He moved his forehead to mine and breathed with me, his intense gaze on my mouth. He hadn't kissed me once since I stepped inside his domain, but he somehow excited me in other intimate ways. His eyes alone touched me everywhere, made me feel things with just their piercing gaze. "I love this..." His hand snaked over my ass and to the curve in my back. His fingers felt the top of my ass to the middle of my spine.

My fingers dug into his shoulders. "I love this." How could I say anything like that to a man like him? How could I feel this burning chemistry between us? I shouldn't desire him. I shouldn't feel myself get wet when I sat on his dick. I should be demanding to be set free.

He pressed his mouth to mine and kissed me slowly, his large hands exploring my body with their callused edges. His kiss was gentle but contained the restrained desire he always showed. He breathed with me, sucking my bottom lip, and then giving me his tongue. The stubble on his chin was already starting to return after not shaving for a few days, so it brushed against my soft cheek as our mouths moved together.

His muscular arms wrapped around my waist and pulled me closer to him, acting as steel cages that kept me in place. Warm and hard, it was like having a blanket wrapped around me.

The sound of our moving mouths filled the room, along with the crackling fireplace. I could hear our breathing get deeper and louder as our heat levels started to rise. I felt his hands grip me tighter, felt his cock throb underneath me.

One of his hands circled over my ass until his fingers met my clit. He kept kissing me as his fingers massaged my nub, making me breathe harder and my hips rock slightly. I realized I was starting to grind against his fingers, loving the way they were touching me.

Just the way I liked to touch myself.

He sucked on my bottom lip and rubbed me harder, making me grip his biceps just to remain steady. He ended our kiss and watched my expression, his eyes full of the same arousal as mine. His fingers slid back to my entrance, and he felt the pool of moisture that immediately smeared across them. A masculine moan came from his throat the second he felt my arousal right in his hand.

I was too turned on to be ashamed. I'd had that big cock twice, and now I looked forward to it. I craved the stretching he gave me, the intense fullness no other man could provide. He was thick like a tree trunk, but I'd always liked a challenge.

He lifted me up his body then pointed the head of his cock at my entrance before he slowly pushed me down his length. It took him a second to get his thick crown inside me, to push through my tight slit and begin the journey into my wet and tight cunt. He moaned when he was halfway inside, his eyes closing for a brief moment as he clenched his jaw.

He looked so hot when he did that.

I moved farther down, managing to get his entire length inside me, even if it hurt a little bit. I stretched my legs wider apart and hooked my ankles over his thighs. His balls were at my ass and his warm body suddenly flushed with heat. It was unmistakable how wet I was…because he was easier to get inside that time.

He pressed his face close to mine then dug his hand into my hair. He didn't kiss me, but he examined my face with the scorching intensity that made me tremble. His fat cock was inside me, and now he possessed me in a way he never had before. He claimed me deeper, harder. He was making me pay for my freedom, making me pay for being allowed to live. "This pussy…Jesus." He crushed his mouth over mine and gave me a hard kiss, a searing kind that made my fingertips light on fire. He ended it just as quickly and then guided my hips up. "Fuck me, baby."

I pressed my hands against his chest as an anchor and moved up and down, riding his big cock from tip to base. I had to work my legs and ass more because he was bigger than average, but I didn't mind the exertion. I loved the way it felt inside me, to feel so much blood stretched inside my pussy.

He rested against the headboard and watched me, wearing that concentrated expression that made him look innately sexy. There was a shadow under his jaw, and his chest rose and fell with his deep breaths.

He promised he would make me forget about all the boys I'd ever been with, and I wanted to make him forget all the women he bedded before me, not because I was possessive or jealous, but because I wanted to have my own power.

So I ran my fingers through my hair as I rode him, played with my tits, and touched myself in ways that would excite any man. I looked him in the eye and made the quiet noises men loved to hear.

His jaw clenched harder and harder, his resistance waning. His cock thickened in me a little further. "Damn."

I brought a finger into my mouth and sucked on it.

His hands moved to my tits as he watched me, palming them with his enormous hands. My average size tits felt small in comparison.

I'd never done this before, but I wanted to impress him. I wanted him under my thumb, to know I was a much bigger woman than he realized. I brought my wet finger to my backside and slipped it inside, moaning when I felt the intrusion.

His body stopped grinding against me, and he sucked in a deep breath. His eyes intensified, shocked by what I'd just done. This time, when he moaned, he sounded more like a bear than a man. "You're fucking with me."

"Is it working?" I kept riding his cock, pushing that thickness inside me and smearing my cream all over him. I held on to his shoulder for balance, my face just inches from his. I could feel his breath fall on me.

He only moaned in response.

I kept riding his dick with my finger in my ass, feeling his breaths come out shakier. He was barely holding on, wanting to come much sooner than he anticipated.

I wanted to come too, but I also wanted to prove a point. He was so arrogant, and I would love to put him in his place—just once.

But he resisted and kept rocking into me from underneath. He grabbed my hips and started to guide me differently, forcing me to rub my clit right against his pelvic bone. The stimulation tested my resistance.

I didn't want to come, but I also did want to come.

And since I'd never come as hard as I did when his dick was inside me, I let it happen.

And it was so fucking good.

Like the Fourth of July between my legs. I screamed in his face, lost control of my thrusts, and dug my nails so deeply into his skin I left marks behind. My pussy nearly broke his dick with the constriction, and I writhed uncontrollably like I lost all control over my body.

It was even better than last time.

When I opened my eyes to look at him again, he wasn't gloating. That intense expression had deepened, and his hands gripped me with more intensity. His body wanted to slip away and join me in the throes of passion, but he hung on, wanting to keep going because he was a stubborn man who didn't fail to prove a point.

"Baby." Whenever he said my pet name, he said it with such masculine possessiveness. I never let any other man call me that, and Bones was the first one who refused to listen. "You're one hell of a woman."

"You haven't seen anything yet." I turned my body around, keeping his dick inside me as I faced the other way. My ass was turned toward him, and I kept grinding against his cock as I fingered myself deep and harder, making sure I kept my back arched and my posture right.

He heaved a deep breath in frustration. "Fuck. Me."

I held on to his muscled thigh as I moved his dick in and out of me. I moved harder, picking up the pace and working up a serious sweat. His dick was so long I had to work my thighs to raise myself up and sheathe him over and over. I pressed my finger deep inside me, knowing he was staring at every little thing I did.

When I felt his cock thicken inside me just a little more, I knew I won.

He gripped my hips and pulled me down his length until I was sitting on him. Then he came loudly, his cock pulsing inside me as he released all his seed.

My face was turned away, so I didn't have to hide my expression out of shame. I didn't have to pretend not to enjoy the feeling of all his come filling me until I was completely stretched apart. I closed my eyes and enjoyed our come mixing together.

He rested his forehead against the back of my neck, his hands still gripping my hips. He breathed deeply, working through the intense emotion that just rocked him from head to toe. He pressed a kiss to the back of my neck as his cock slowly softened inside me. His fingers dug a little deeper before he finally released me. "You need to work on stretching that asshole more. My dick will be next."

6

Bones

Vanessa made good on her word.

She really was addicting.

I hadn't gotten that much enjoyment out of a woman before. The sex was good, but once I was finished, the drive was usually gone. I was a man with needs, so lots of sex was a part of my life. But it wasn't ever with the same person.

Until now.

I fucked her once, but immediately afterward, I wanted her again.

I told myself that my obsession came from the context of the situation. She was the daughter of my

131

mortal enemy and stuffing my come between her legs felt forbidden. It felt like a form of revenge, a way to get off without actually killing her. If Crow Barsetti knew what I was doing, it would send him on a terrifying rampage.

Especially since his daughter enjoyed it.

I had to release her back into the wild soon, but I had no intention of letting her go. She would still be my prisoner because I had the kind of power to control someone without being in the same room or the same city. I only had a few more days before one of her parents called to check in on her.

I had to make sure everything was ready by then.

Richard knocked before he stepped into my office. "Sir, I just wanted to let you know Vanessa is outside."

I immediately turned in my chair and looked out the large window. "What is she doing?"

"Looks like she's playing in the snow. Just wanted you to be aware." He walked out again.

The storm had passed, and it was a sunny day. The snow had settled, and the sunlight made it ten degrees warmer than it usually was. I wasn't stupid enough to underestimate my opponent. No matter how much she liked to fuck me, I knew she would betray me the second the opportunity came up.

I'd do the same to her.

I pulled on my boots and jacket before I went outside. She was in the back, dressed in snow gear she must have found in her closet. With a thick jacket, water-resistant pants, and gloves, she was building a snowman. She made the bottom snowball then worked to construct the next piece that went on top. On the ground beside her were carrots, olives, and a piece of wood she would use to make the face.

I stared at her for a second, unable to believe what I was looking at. This woman had been kidnapped and almost murdered, but she was outside on a nice day making a snowman. She reminded me of a child visiting her grandparents on Christmas.

I came closer to her, my boots crunching against the snow.

She looked up when she noticed me. "Does it look like I'm running?"

"Would you tell me if you were?"

She shrugged. "Good point." She finished the second ball and then placed it on top of the bottom one.

I slipped my hands in my pockets and watched her.

"You don't need to babysit me, Bones. If I were going to run, I would have made my move already."

"Unless you realized the garage is locked with a code and the path down to the road is completely covered in snow."

She grinned as she rubbed her hands together and wiped the snow from her gloves. "Alright, you got me."

Her honesty heightened my attraction to her.

"Then there really is no reason for you to be out here, then."

"I can think of one." I placed my body in between her and the snowman, and I stared at her lips like I could claim them with just my look.

She cocked her head slightly, holding my gaze with her fiery expression. "You want to build a snowman with me?"

"I want a kiss first."

She pressed her lips tightly together then rolled her eyes. "I'm not giving you anything. I'll kiss you when I fuck you—"

My hand dug into her hair, and I crushed my mouth to hers, kissing her in the snow. I took charge of the kiss, forcing her lips to move with mine. Our breath escaped as vapor into the dry air. The back of her neck was warm because her hair protected her skin, and my fingers latched on to it as I deepened the kiss.

She was a big smartass, but the second my mouth was on hers, she was completely cooperative.

I pulled away but kept my face close to hers. "You'll kiss me when I say so." I turned away then kneeled down to the snow. With my bare hands, I constructed a small snow ball. I lifted it and placed it on top of the snowman.

Vanessa chucked a snowball at the side of my face, the cold ice striking me right on the cheek.

I turned back to her, my eyes narrowed. "You don't want to play that game with me."

"Come on, I'm a good shot." She wore a playful smile on her face, the sunlight highlighting the beautiful color of her skin. Her eyes were full of life despite her current circumstances. Nothing could keep this woman down for long.

"If you were a good shot, I'd be dead right now."

She rolled her eyes. "Guns are different. I don't use them often. I only shot someone one time before— and I didn't miss then."

The playful mood immediately evaporated when I heard what she said. "You shot and killed someone?"

"Yeah." She pulled out the carrot and shoved it into the center of the snowman's face. She brushed off the conversation like it was casual, like the current circumstances we were in was completely normal.

My attention was only on her, not the snowman she was making. "Who and why?"

"My future sister-in-law had some asshole who was obsessed with her. So he kidnapped me and said he would only set me free if my brother released his girl-friend. He wanted to make a trade. But I ran for it instead, got a gun, and shot one of his henchmen in the skull. I didn't have time to check, but I'm pretty sure he died."

Pride rushed through me, pleased that Vanessa was smart and cunning enough to escape her captors. She didn't think twice before she claimed a man's life. Life wasn't as simple as people thought it was, and those who would rather die than take a life deserved to die anyway. Vanessa acted quickly and got herself out of a bad situation. She tried to do the same with me, but I was a much harder opponent. "Did you kill the guy who took you?"

"No. My mom did. She had a gun, but she strangled him with a rope. I've never seen my mom look like that...look so terrifying."

Had she been as vicious with my father?

Vanessa must have picked up on my mood because her gaze shifted to my face, full of concern. "What?"

I stared at her beautiful face and did my best to combat the rage burning in my blood. I was an orphan because of Vanessa's family. I had everything stripped from me. I was punished for a crime that occurred when I wasn't even alive. It didn't matter how attracted I was to this woman. The lines between us couldn't be blurred. She was my enemy. She would always be my enemy. "Nothing."

———

WE HAD DINNER TOGETHER.

Vanessa must have known I was in a bad mood because she didn't make conversation. She drank her wine and cut into her chicken, being so quiet it was like she wasn't even there.

I stared at her hard across the table, my jaw tense throughout the entire meal. This woman was so beautiful but so deadly to me. She had the life I should have had, loved by both of her parents with a life of luxury. While she was going to recitals and private school, I was in an orphanage or living on the street. She had it easy. I had it fucking hard.

"You need to let it go."

I stopped chewing for a second, surprised by what she said. I finished my food before I swallowed. "Meaning?"

"You've been pissed since I mentioned my mom earlier. It's the only explanation for your mood swing."

"It's not a mood swing. I'm always ticked."

"Well, you're more ticked than usual."

"I hate your mother. You think that's ever going to

change?" I gripped my fork so hard it hurt my fingertips. "Fuck me as good as you want, but my hatred will never settle. Your family ruined my life. They will pay for what they did."

She stilled at my words, her own anger slowly filling the room. "Be careful what you say, Bones. You know I'll defend their honor to my final breath, even turn this delicious dinner into a knife fight."

"You'd be dead before you could even grab your weapon." I picked up my scotch and took a long drink.

"Don't underestimate me."

"I don't." She might come in a small package, but she was packed with intelligence and strength. She proved to me that she was a formidable opponent. I knew it the moment I electrocuted her in the neck and she didn't stop running.

Badass.

She turned her gaze down to her food. "Once you let your anger go, you'll finally be happy."

"I'll never be happy. I've never been happy. I don't even know what that word means."

"Because you've never given yourself the opportunity."

Even if I did, I'd been through too much. I'd suffered more than she could understand. Living on the streets left me begging for food. People took advantage of my position and beat the shit out of me just to take the few euros I collected from strangers. I toughened up at the age of twelve, learning to survive with nothing. Before I turned eighteen, I was a force to be reckoned with. "You've had a nice life. A nice family. You'll never understand what I've been through. You can't even conceive of it."

"Then show me."

I finally loosened my hand on my fork and returned to eating. "You don't give a damn about me and you shouldn't. If given the chance, I would kill both of your parents right in front of you. So don't waste any time pitying me or pretending to pity me. I hate you. You hate me. Let's leave it at that."

———

I FUCKED HER FROM BEHIND, gripping both of her shoulders as I slammed my fat cock inside her.

Despite the tense conversations we had that day, she was soaking wet and my cock was rock-hard.

We hated each other, but that didn't stop us from wanting to fuck each other's brains out.

The chemistry was natural. I desired her, and she desired me. She was the sexiest woman on the planet, and I knew she looked at me like I was the kind of guy she'd always wanted. If we'd met under different circumstances, at a bar or a restaurant, we would have found each other.

And fucked just like this.

She came around my dick twice, just as I intended. I wanted her to hate everything about me except my dick. I wanted my cock to have unquestionable power over her, to bring her to her knees every single time.

I pumped my come inside her when I was finished, my white seed seeping out of her because there was too much of it to fit inside her. I gripped her ass when I finished, my cock twitching at the very end. I let my length soften a little before I pulled out of her then lay on my bed. I stared at the ceiling, listening to the fireplace die out as my heartbeat slowly went back to normal.

She lay beside me, keeping several inches between us so we weren't touching.

I didn't kiss her that night.

It was pure fucking, all carnal and passion.

She broke the silence once our breathing returned to normal. "When are you going to let me go?"

I kept my eyes on the ceiling, my hand tucked under my head. "When I feel like it."

"My mother is going to call any day…"

"Don't give a damn." Now I wanted them to come after her. Once they were on the front steps, I would slit her throat. Killing her would be the perfect revenge, and now it sounded appealing once more.

But I knew I could never do it.

There was something about Vanessa that softened my resolve. I respected her too much to kill her. We needed more women like her in the world, women who could hold their own against a man twice their size. If only my mother had been more like her, she might still be alive. Perhaps that was why I'd become so fond of her. She told me she'd been kidnapped before and she got away.

Why couldn't my mother have gotten away?

If she were alive right now, I'd be taking care of her. She'd have a nice house and everything she needed.

But some asshole killed her and left her in a dumpster.

Vanessa turned on her side then propped herself on her elbow, looking down at me as her hair fell toward the sheets. "What's your real name?"

I turned my head slightly toward her, my eyes looking at the beautiful woman staring down at me. "You know my name."

"I know that isn't the real one, though."

"It's the only one you need to know."

She scooted closer to me until her leg was tucked between mine and her hand was on my chest.

I just filled her with pussy with so much come, but when she touched me like this, it sent another wave of pleasure through me. Her skin was so warm, and her fingertips felt so soft against my hard chest. Her hair fell down toward my face, so my fingers slid through the strands and kept it pinned back. I could stare at this woman forever. Sometimes, when I looked at her eyes,

I forgot her roots. I pretended she was no one, just a woman I stumbled upon during one of my adventures.

My eyes moved to her shoulder, to the scar that was still slightly fresh. It was obviously a bullet hole. I noticed it the first time I saw her naked on the blue plastic. In that moment, I intended to kill her, so I never asked about it. "What's this from?" My hand grazed over the injury, feeling the slight bumps.

"When I ran from that guy, he shot me." She talked about her past with simplicity, like it had no hold over her anymore. She wasn't in emotional distress or suffering from post-traumatic stress. She was accepting of her past, even the ugly scar that destroyed the softness of her skin.

I raised my head and kissed the skin, kissed the scar tissue like it was her lips. "I'm sorry." I returned my head to the bed, my fingers still gliding over the area.

"You shouldn't be sorry."

"But I am."

Her hand moved to my arm, to the area where she shot me with her bullet. "I want to apologize for shooting you, but I can't…" She ran her fingers over it, where the ink had been destroyed because the bullet pierced the skin.

"I don't expect you to. You did the right thing." My hand glided down the steep curve in her back to her ass. My hands were obsessed with her body, obsessed with touching her. I gripped her ass cheek then slid down her long leg. "But you should have aimed better and killed me."

She smiled slightly. "I don't know if I agree with that. You didn't kill me, after all…"

"Doesn't mean I won't."

She held my gaze, her confidence shining like a beacon. "I don't think you will."

I wanted to tell her she was wrong. I wanted to force her to her knees on the floor and execute her right then and there. I could shove her hand into the fireplace and watch her burn alive. It wouldn't be my first time. But I kept my mouth shut and didn't say anything, knowing I would look like a fool because I wouldn't follow through with it. "You're a smart woman, baby. It's one of the things I like about you. So don't drop your guard around me. Don't assume you're safe with me. Because if the time comes when

I need to end you, I want you to fight me every step of the way."

Her eyes hardened as she stared at me. "I never said I felt safe around you. I've never dropped my guard. And if there ever comes a time when I can be free or betray you, I will. But that doesn't change what I said. I don't think you'll kill me. In your heart, you know I'm not guilty of the crime my family inflicted on yours. I wasn't even alive at the time, and neither were you. I'm an innocent woman who was just in the wrong place at the wrong time...like your mother. I find it hard to believe you would do something like that."

When you possessed as much hatred as I did, nothing was logical anymore. Everything was about bloodshed and revenge. Innocent people died every day in the crossfires. Vanessa was no different. "All is fair in love and war."

———

I WAS HARD when I woke up every morning, my big dick lying against my stomach. It happened every single day since I hit puberty. And now when I woke up, Vanessa was cuddled right into my side. When she fell asleep, she was always at the far end of the bed. But she always got cold in the middle of the night and migrated her way toward me without even realizing it.

I took one look at her, her face well rested after a long night of sleep, and rolled her to her back. The second I saw this beautiful woman beside me, I wanted to be buried inside her. It was how I wanted to get my morning started every single day, giving my come to Vanessa Barsetti.

She stirred as I moved her but didn't wake up fully. She was used to doing this every morning, so now her legs spread automatically, and she hooked her arms over my shoulders and held on.

I sank my cock inside her, moving slowly until I was sheathed to my balls. My face moved into her neck, and I started to thrust, pushing my dick inside her over and over. She was wet in the morning, probably because her body was getting used to taking my cock at the same time every day.

She moaned with me, her throat still dry from being asleep.

I loved fucking her like this, half asleep. My cock was more sensitive in the morning, so she felt even better than usual. I grunted with my movements, smelling her hair. My body rubbed right against her clit because my body rested on hers, so I usually made her come in record time.

She loved morning sex as much as I did.

She clawed at my back and moaned directly into my ear, quieter than usual but still climaxing hard. Her teeth sank into my shoulder and her pussy tightened around me, begging my cock to give her the seed she loved so much.

I came right after, finishing us both off in less than two minutes. I dumped all my come inside her before I rolled over onto my back again. My eyes closed, and I caught my breath, still reeling from the orgasm I just had.

Fuck, I could do this every day.

Vanessa turned on her side and snuggled into me, her pussy full of new come and the come from last night.

Damn, she was always full of me.

Her arm wrapped around my waist, and she rested her head on my shoulder.

My fingers slowly dragged down her side, feeling her

smooth skin. My fingertips were callused, but I could still feel her intimate details.

She sighed against me, satisfied and relaxed. "Morning…"

"Morning."

She moved closer into me, her body all over mine.

I liked it—a lot. My hand moved to her thigh as it stretched across my body. "You're studying art?" I knew a bit about her from my research. She was going to school in Milan with art as her discipline. She didn't exhibit any specific traits that identified her as an artist, but I wouldn't be surprised if she had the talent to paint a masterpiece. She never failed to surprise me.

"Yes." Her small hand rested right on my sternum. "I want to be a painter."

"What do you paint?"

"Everything."

"Be more specific."

She tilted her head up so her eyes could meet mine. "Well, my last piece was an image of my parents working in the vineyards together. Husband and wife cultivating the soil. It's supposed to represent Italian culture, of the foundation and loyalty of family."

Anytime her family was mentioned, I became angry. But this time, I controlled my rage. It was too early in the morning, and I just had an amazing orgasm with my cock buried inside this woman. "So you want to paint professionally?"

"I guess. There's not really any such thing. I just want to be good enough so people will buy my work. Maybe I can open a gallery or something. But making art is about connecting with people. I have to create something that moves people. If I fail to do that, then no one will be interested in my pieces. It can't just look nice. It has to be something that someone wants for many years."

"Has anyone ever bought one of your paintings?"

"Just my parents," she answered. "And they would buy anything I make, so they don't really count."

She clearly had a perfect childhood, judging by the way she spoke so highly of her parents. They had a nice, quiet life in Tuscany, working their successful winery. I'd never started an honest business, choosing to remain in the dark and make my money in horrid ways.

"You have a lot of artwork in your house."

"Richard picked it out."

"They're nice," she said. "I've looked at them many times. I noticed you don't have a picture of you or your mom anywhere."

I turned my face back to the ceiling and never commented.

After a tense moment of silence, she sat up and pulled her hair from her face. "I should get up and take a shower. I'm really hungry and can't wait for breakfast." For a small woman, she had a big appetite. She always ate everything at our meals and complimented Richard on the dishes he prepared.

"Make sure you get enough to eat. We're leaving today."

She turned her gaze back to me, the hope obvious.

I didn't like that look. I wanted her to stay at my house with me forever. I wanted to keep her as my prisoner forever. If she didn't have such a powerful family, I probably would. But under the circumstances, I was risking too much. If I killed her, that would be one thing. But her family would kill me, and if I never finished what I started, I would have accomplished nothing. "Don't be too excited."

———

ONCE THE SNOW was shoveled away, we got into my truck and left the property.

I handed her phone back to her. I had it in my office, constantly charging so it wouldn't die. I looked through her text messages, seeing some of her friends check in with her. A few guys texted her too.

I didn't care for that.

She took the phone with shaky hands, rubbing her thumbs over the screen like she couldn't believe it was really in her possession again.

Some things were too good to be true, including this.

I pulled onto the icy road and then began the journey back to Milan. She was in the clothes she arrived in, but now they'd been cleaned. The heater was on so she wouldn't freeze, but I kept the radio off.

I preferred silence.

She finally asked the question on her mind. "You're taking me back and you've given me my phone…how do you know I won't just round up my family to kill you? I know where you live."

"You know of *one* place where I live." I drove with one hand on the steering wheel, the other resting on the windowsill. My eyes were on the road, but I could see her in my peripheral vision. "I have many places."

"Do you have a place in Milan?"

I grinned. "Why do you want to know?"

"Just curious."

"Yes. I have a place there."

"Well…you didn't answer my question."

I was taking a gamble here, but the reward outweighed the risk. "You won't say anything to them."

"Why wouldn't I?" she asked. "You didn't kill me, but you've made it abundantly clear my family is your blood enemy. While I'm grateful I'm still alive right now, I will do anything I can to protect my family. This is a stupid thing to say, but the second I talk to them, I'm telling them everything."

That didn't surprise me. I'd judge her if she did anything less. "You're missing a piece of the story."

"What piece?" she asked.

I followed the curves of the road and headed down the mountain. Lake Garda was beautiful right now, calm and flat while the mountain peaks behind it were covered in white caps. I thrived in the winter and despised the humid heat of summer—along with the tourists. "Keep this to yourself, and I promise I won't touch any member of your family—that includes Sapphire, who isn't family yet."

"How did you know her name?"

I chuckled. "Baby, I know everything about my enemies." Plus, she was on TV everywhere. The media thought she was the most stunning woman in the world, but I'd seen a different woman in lingerie —and she was way better.

"And that's it?" she asked incredulously. "You'll just drop your revenge like that?"

"Not quite. I am getting my revenge, just in a different way."

"How?"

"Because you're mine." I felt her head immediately turn my way once she heard the words.

"What?" she asked quietly. "What does that mean?"

"It means you're mine. You have your own life, and I have mine. I've got a lot of shit to do, and I can't be with you all the time. I travel a lot for work. Sometimes I'll be gone for weeks at a time. But I'm free to come and go as I please, to fuck you before you wake up in the morning and to fuck you before you go to sleep at night. You're a prisoner—but you're free at the same time."

"You've got to be kidding me."

I grinned when I listened to the terror in her voice. "No."

"That's ridiculous. I'll have a boyfriend eventually."

"You can have a boyfriend. But when I stop by, he's forgotten."

"I'm not a cheater," she snapped.

"Then don't have a boyfriend."

"I'm going to fall in love with someone and get married."

"And when that day comes, the blood war is back on. You can break our arrangement anytime you want, but the second you do, I'll be coming after your family."

She stared out the window and sighed under her breath, livid.

I was enjoying every second of it.

"You can't do that," she whispered.

"Would you rather I kill you?" I questioned. "This is the only other option. I have you as my prisoner, and I'm punishing your parents without them even knowing about it. I know you'll comply because it's the best way to keep everyone safe. And it's not like you don't get other things out of it…"

"Fuck you," she snapped.

"Baby, you aren't going to want another man after having me. The sex won't be nearly as good, and he won't be nearly as big. You're used to the best now, to a man who knows how to please a woman. And once you've had a taste of that…you'll never go back."

"Your arrogance is disgusting."

"But it makes you want me more anyway."

She sighed again and looked out the window. She turned quiet, her arms folded over her chest. Her legs were crossed, and her phone sat on her lap. She didn't say anything else on the drive. She knew the only way to get out of this situation was to kill me herself.

And I knew she would try.

I was looking forward to it.

———

WE PULLED up to her apartment, and I killed the engine.

She didn't ask how I knew where she lived, but I knew she was wondering.

We walked to her front door, and she got the door unlocked before we walked inside. Her apartment was small, perfect for a single person. She had a small living room with two couches and a TV. Down the hall was her bedroom and her bathroom.

I glanced around, seeing the brightly colored furniture and the vase of flowers that had died while she'd been away for the past few days.

She set her purse and phone on the entryway table then crossed her arms over her chest. Her lips were pressed tightly together, and her smoldering attitude filled the space between us.

I took a look around, moving through the limited space. She had pictures of her family on one of her shelves, images of her and Conway along with her parents. My eyes didn't linger for long before I turned away.

"I have a question."

I turned around and faced her, seeing the anger in her eyes. I'd seen her enraged before, but this look was different. I knew she felt powerless, frustrated. She always managed to get the upper hand in the worst situations, but this time, there was no solution. The first person she would turn to for help was her father—but now he was off-limits. "Yes, baby?"

Her eyes flared a little when she heard the nickname. "I have to know…that night in the alleyway…was that a coincidence? Or did you plan for all of that to happen?"

It was purely coincidental. I was a lucky son-of-a-bitch that was in the right place at the right time. She was the unlucky one. And I wanted to keep that information from her, to make her feel unsafe. But I also vowed to be honest with her, and since she was such a respectable woman, I didn't want to go back on my word. So I chose not to give her the answer. "It doesn't matter. This is where we are, and any speculation on the past won't change it."

"Why don't you just tell me?"

"Because not knowing makes it more interesting."

"No. It's just another way for you to have power over me."

She was absolutely right. "And I love having power over you." There was no greater feeling than making a powerful woman like Vanessa submit so obediently. Only a very powerful man could get a woman like her to listen.

And that man was me.

"This can't go on forever," she said. "I won't be your slave forever."

"You're right. Eventually, I'll get tired of you." I found her mesmerizing now, with those full lips and beautiful eyes. I thought she was the most gorgeous woman I'd ever been with. I hadn't even started to do the dark things I wanted. But like any other woman, she would lose her allure and someone else would take her place. "I just don't know when that will be."

"And then what?" she demanded. "You'll kill my family then?"

I wouldn't stop until both of her parents were dead and buried in the Tuscan soil they loved so much. "Yes. So if I were you, I would make sure I don't get tired of you."

7

Vanessa

My life was no longer the same.

I was back in my apartment, but the four walls that surrounded me didn't make me feel safe anymore. Knuckles had broken in and smacked me around, and now a viler man had turned me into a prisoner in my own home.

What the hell was I going to do?

I'd witnessed this man's savage ways, and I knew he wanted nothing more than to torture my parents and kill them. The only thing stopping him was his obsession with my pussy. I wanted to protect my family by keeping my mouth shut, but if they knew my freedom had been stripped away like this, they would be devastated.

I only had one choice.

I had to kill Bones myself.

I could get a gun from my father. All I had to do was say I wanted it for protection. He'd always encouraged me to have one for safety, but I always insisted I didn't need one.

Looks like I was wrong about that.

I had knives, but stabbing Bones wouldn't be so easy. He was a huge man. It would be easy to miss, especially when I was that close to him.

My only option was a gun.

After he dropped me off, he left. He said he had work to do, and he would be gone for a few days. But before he left, he inserted a tracker into my ankle. That way he could see where I was at all times.

I fought him hard when he pushed the needle into my skin, but there was no use. He was too strong.

He was the strongest man I'd ever encountered.

Definitely stronger than my father and my uncle. Even stronger than Conway and Carter.

Fuck, how did I get into this?

I tried to keep calm by remembering Bones didn't kill me. I could be dead and that video sent to my parents. I escaped that threat, so I had something to be thankful for. Not all hope was lost.

I would find a way out of this.

Because I was a Barsetti—and Barsettis don't give up.

———

I MISSED NEARLY a whole week of school because Bones had me hidden away, and the day I finally went to class was the last one before school ended for the winter break. Christmas was around the corner, and I hadn't even considered shopping.

I was broke anyway.

I usually made things for my family, and hopefully, I had enough time to pull something together. The painting I'd been working on for class was never finished, so I wrapped it up and carried it home through the snow.

I returned to the warmth of my apartment and set it on the easel. I bought some other supplies, so I could do some artwork during my break. I considered making a painting for my whole family, an image of us gathered together for the holidays. But if I were to finish it, I would have to start now.

I set my things down and then heard my phone ring.

It was my mom.

I hadn't spoken to her since Bones captured me. She had no idea what I'd been through. I had to hide it from her, but she could usually tell when I was trying to hide something. And now that I knew what had happened to her, I'd have to keep that bottled up too.

Every time I thought about what happened to her, I wanted to cry.

My mama.

I cleared my throat then answered the phone. "Hey, Mama."

"Hey, Vanessa. How are things? I'm sorry I haven't called sooner. We've just been busy with the house."

"No big deal. I know you guys are busy. Getting ready for Christmas?"

"Yep. Your father hung up the lights and everything is looking nice. Lars can't get around as easily as he used to, so we're working together to get the house in shape. Aunt Adelina's parents are coming too, so we want them to feel welcome."

"Oh great. I love seeing them." I sat on the couch, thinking about the small tracker planted inside my ankle.

"So when are you coming home?"

"Probably in a few days. I need to finish up some stuff around here."

"How did the end of your semester go?"

"Great." I missed the last few days and took my finals without studying...so I hoped I passed. It didn't really matter if I didn't. "Just glad it's over."

"Your father and I figured you were busy. I remember how that used to be."

"Yeah, a million years ago," I teased.

"Oh, shut up," she said with a laugh. "I'm not that old."

"You certainly don't look it."

"That's much better. Well, I'll let you go. Love you, sweetheart."

It killed me that I couldn't tell her what was really

going on in my life, that I had been trapped with the biggest enemy to our family. But if I said anything and he found out about it, he would strike them first before they had a chance to do anything in retaliation. And I wanted to tell her that I knew what happened to her…and that I was there if she ever wanted to talk about it. But I kept my mouth shut. "Love you too, Mama."

————

I PAINTED all day by the light of the window, and when it turned dark, I went out with a few friends to the bars. I saw a lot of good-looking guys, and a few even made passes at me, but knowing I was in a twisted situation made me blow them off.

They shouldn't get involved with me.

I went home before midnight, slipped off my heels by the door, and then headed to my bedroom in my cocktail dress. Bones had been gone for three days. I didn't hear anything from him, and I wasn't sure when he would stop by.

I didn't want to see his face, not ever again, but I did notice the changes in my body.

The changes in my hormones.

I was wet every night and every morning, and my mind drifted back to the memories I had of him. I might despise him for the monster he was, but there was no denying my body craved his.

I missed that good sex every morning and every night.

I'd never been in a long-term relationship before, so having sex with the same person at regular intervals was new to me. I hooked up with my other boyfriends whenever the time arose, but we didn't shack up together for days on end.

The shame killed me.

How could I want a man who held a knife to my throat? Who kidnapped me for days? Who wanted to kill my family?

I knew it was just physical, and if I could kill him I would, but that didn't make me feel better about it.

Only worse.

I was just about to peel off my dress and get ready for bed when I heard the front door. It opened and shut

PENELOPE SKY

casually, like someone had every right to walk into my apartment like they owned it.

I knew it was him.

The door was locked, but he obviously had a key. A key I never gave to him.

I stilled in my bedroom, holding my breath as I listened to his footsteps on the hardwood floor. The steps became louder as he migrated to the bedroom. The sound indicated his heavy mass, his thick presence as he filled the apartment.

I didn't turn around to face the door, knowing he was standing there staring at me. I could feel his crystal-blue eyes pierce through my body. He was staring at me up and down, looking at my frame in the tight black dress. My breathing halted because I could feel him, and with anticipation, I felt him come closer to me.

His footsteps were light, but he was so close I could hear everything.

Then I smelled his scent of snow, pine, and cologne mixed together.

I felt his heat afterward, his desire. He didn't need to

168

touch me to express his intentions. I could feel his arousal like I was standing next to a raging fire.

He finally closed the space between us by pressing his chest against my back. His lips moved to my ear, and his hands glided down my body, starting at my waist and sliding down my thighs. He reached the end of the dress then balled it in his fingertips, gathering it up until he slowly pulled it over my ass, revealing my cheeks in my thong. He left the dress at my waistline and breathed directly into my ear. "Fuck, I missed you."

I closed my eyes and held my breath, feeling my body immediately betray me the second his hands were on me. My nipples hardened in the dress, and I imagined the monster standing behind me, picturing the way he looked as he held me in his arms.

His hand snaked around my waist and down my belly. He aimed for my panty line, and once he slipped inside the fabric, he kept going until he reached my clit. He rubbed it just the way he did before, doing it better than I did when I was alone. He used two fingers to rub me good, forcing me to breathe deeply as I enjoyed the pleasure. His fingers picked up the arousal oozing from my cunt, the wetness that was already there before he walked in the door.

But he knew it was for him. "You missed me too…"

Shame was still in my blood, but the arousal was much stronger. Now all I could think about was that big dick deep inside me. I went out to the bars hoping to meet a nice guy to have a fun evening with, but in the back of my mind, I knew I wanted sex like this.

Sex with this monster.

He gripped the back of my panties and pulled them down my ass as his fingers continued to rub me. He kept going until he moved to his knees and pulled them the rest of the way. His lips brushed against my legs on the way down.

I opened my eyes and gripped his shoulder for balance as he helped me out of my thong.

When he rose to his feet, he lifted me with him. Like I was lighter than air, he carried me to bed. He set me down, leaving my dress on and bunched around my waist. He stood at the foot of my bed and pulled his t-shirt over his head, revealing his chiseled physique along with all his ink. "Spread your legs."

My knees were pressed together, not out of rejection, but because it was the automatic position I took once I was on the bed. I kept my thighs pressed tightly together as I stared at him, watching him move to his jeans next. I was so wet for him that I could feel the moisture smear across the inside of my thighs. I simply did it out of defiance, wishing I didn't feel this way about a man so evil.

"Don't make me ask you again." He undid his jeans and pushed them down with his boxers, revealing his fat cock. He was already oozing from the crown, just the way I was oozing for him all over my bed.

My legs finally came away, opening.

"Farther."

I parted my ankles wider and pulled my knees back, making my body completely open to him. He could see all the details of my pussy, see the way my arousal gleamed in the lamplight. I held myself up on my elbows, self-conscious about my position but also turned on by the way he stared at me.

Like he'd never seen anything sexier in his life.

He grabbed his shaft and stroked himself with his fingers, pumping himself as one knee hit the bed. The entire mattress shifted under his weight. His muscled thighs bulged with his movements, and the rest of his muscles tightened as he came closer to me on the bed, his dick hard and ready to go.

Instead of shoving his dick inside me and fucking me right away, he held himself at my knees, his face above my pussy. "How do you want me to fuck you, baby?"

I didn't give a damn right now. All I knew was I wanted him inside me as quickly as possible. I hadn't had a climax in three days, and I was used to having two every single day. Regardless of what position he took me in, he would make me come. I had complete faith that this man would deliver every single time he was inside me.

He was right. He did raise my standards for all men. I could have found someone else tonight, but I didn't want to gamble on the possibility of fucking someone without getting off. But with Bones, I knew he would always make me come so damn hard.

My hands gripped his shoulders. "I don't care."

"Yes, you do." He moved his face closer to mine, getting close enough that he could kiss me if he wanted to. "Tell me. Tell me how you've wanted me to fuck you for the past three days. Tell me how I can satisfy this wet pussy. Tell me what I can do to be worthy of fucking a woman like you."

My thighs automatically wanted to squeeze together in response because his words turned me on even more. He wasn't just anxious to fuck me, but anxious to make me feel good too. He wanted my pussy to tighten around his dick. He wanted the power and the pride. He wanted to keep the reputation he earned—of being a man and not a boy.

"Baby, tell me."

I didn't even care that he called me baby right now. "With your arms locked behind my knees…and your dick as deep as possible…with your lips on mine."

"Slow or hard?"

"So fucking hard."

He moaned then did the unexpected. He relaxed his body on the mattress and then pressed his face between my legs. His mouth immediately began to devour me, kissing me the way only a few men had before.

My head rolled back, and my thighs automatically came together, but his hands locked me in place. He sucked my clit hard then circled it with his big tongue.

He kissed my pussy just the way he kissed my lips, with full possession and obsession.

I was writhing and aching, so close to climaxing already. "Yes…" I felt the burn deep inside my stomach as it inched toward the apex of my thighs. I was going to come, going to explode.

He abruptly pulled away then crawled on top of me.

"Ugh…"

"Don't worry, baby. I never disappoint you, right?"

"No…"

He locked his arms behind my knees just as I asked and leaned over me, his throbbing cock ready to slam inside me. But he paused, as if he were waiting for something.

I clawed at his forearms. "What?"

"Tell me to fuck you."

If I weren't in this sex-crazed fog, I would have told him to fuck off. But my mind was completely lost in the arousal. I wanted his cock inside me. I wanted his kiss on my lips. My body told him exactly what I wanted, but the fact that he was making me say it made it more real. I grabbed his hips and pulled him toward me.

He resisted me. "Say it, baby."

I was still on the verge of coming. I could feel the explosion bubbling between my legs. I grew frustrated waiting. "Shut up and fuck me."

"Please."

I lost my temper and slapped him across the face. "No, asshole. I'm not going to say please. Now fuck me and be appreciative of the fact that you even get to fuck me."

His face moved with the hit, so he slowly turned his face back toward me. His cheek was red because I hit him so hard, but the malicious grin showed the opposite of anger. It seemed to turn him on more, even amuse him. "That's my baby…" He finally shoved his cock into me and slid all the way inside in one swift motion.

"Yes…" My nails dug into his back, and I moaned once I felt that enormous dick stretch me apart. My head moved back to the pillow, and I yanked his face down to mine so I could finally kiss him.

He kissed me hard, his lips tasting like my arousal.

My nails dragged down his back to his ass, and I pulled him deeper inside me, moaning at the same time.

He gave me his tongue, his passion, and everything else. He thrust hard with his hips, taking me more aggressively than usual. I was so soaked that his dick fit inside even better than it ever had before. "Fuck...yes."

I already hit my threshold. I wanted to come before he was even inside me, and now I did with an explosive pulse. Like a shattered star, I came apart into a million pieces. It was so good I thought I might black out in the middle of it. I got tight around his dick, and my nails left trails everywhere they'd been on his skin. I flooded him with more arousal and screamed directly into his mouth, drowning in the pleasure he gave me.

He kept going hard even when I was finished. "See the difference?" he said through his heavy breathing. "This is what it's like to fuck a man, baby. And now you'll never want to fuck another boy again."

I already came, but I knew I was going to come again. I could already feel the arousal building up between my legs. It was a new sensation, something I never felt before. I'd heard about multiple orgasms but never had one in reality. "Yes...fuck me."

He pressed his forehead to mine and hit me deeper. "I'm the only man who is man enough to fuck a woman like you."

———

I WOKE up the next morning in exactly what I was wearing the night before. My dress was still pulled up to my waist, and my panties were on the other side of the room. I didn't sleep under the covers because Bones was warm enough to keep me comfortable throughout the night.

As my eyes opened, the night before came back to me.

We fucked so damn hard.

God, it was so good.

But so fucking bad.

He was naked beside me, a behemoth more than a man. His chest rose and fell at a steady rate, his black ink slightly messed up in the various places he'd been shot or stabbed. I examined them in more detail while he slept, never noticing them before because I never had the chance.

He was usually awake before I was.

I counted three stab wounds and four bullet holes.

Jesus.

He woke up shortly afterward, his cock already hard against his stomach. He had a serious case of morning wood—and he had it every single day. He opened his eyes slowly and stared at the ceiling. It seemed to take him a second to remember where he was.

To remember last night.

He slowly turned toward me, a slight grin on his face.

He was definitely thinking of last night.

I refused to blush. I refused to show weakness. Even though that usually made him want me more.

"Your bed is comfortable."

"Thanks. Sorry it's a queen."

"When you sleep on me like this, it doesn't make a difference." He rolled on top of me, and like every morning when I stayed with him, he pointed his cock at my entrance and slid inside me.

I missed morning sex. I didn't realize how much I missed it until I started to wake up horny every morning.

Like every other time, it was slow because we were both waking up still. Still slightly asleep, our sensations were heightened. Everything felt so much better, more intense. His hand slid into my hair, and he kept me in place as his hips thrust into me.

I came shortly afterward, coming around his dick while his seed was still inside me from the night before.

He came immediately afterward, like he was just waiting for me to finish so he could release himself. He stayed inside me until his cock started to soften. Then he got out of bed. "I'm getting in the shower. I want breakfast when I'm done."

And just like that, the comfortable moment we just had was shattered. "Excuse me?"

He stood by the bed, over six feet of all muscle. "You heard me."

"I'm not cooking for you."

His eyes narrowed. "I cooked for you every day when you stayed with me."

"Uh, no, you didn't."

"I'm the one who paid to have it prepared."

"Asshole, I don't cook. I can barely make eggs. The only thing I can do is make coffee—because I have a coffee machine."

"Then what do you eat every morning?"

"Coffee."

"And?" he pressed.

"And coffee," I repeated.

"When do you eat real food?"

"Lunch time."

"And what do you have then?"

"I pick up something. Same with dinner."

He grabbed his t-shirt from the floor then pulled it over his head. "Then let's go out for breakfast."

I laughed because it was ridiculous. "Yeah, okay…"

He stared me down, his pretty eyes no longer so beautiful. "I'm serious."

"You want to go out in public?" I asked incredulously. "Together?"

"Yes. Now, put something on. But I don't mind if you want to go out like that." He nodded to my dress. "Let the whole world know I fucked you last night. Works for me." He stepped into my bathroom then turned on the faucet.

I couldn't believe I was going out into the real world with this guy.

With this monster.

———

WE WENT to a café down the street from my house. The snow had melted with the sun, but there were still patches of it everywhere. We sat inside by the windows, which were frosted by the corners because it was so cold outside.

A steaming cup of coffee was in front of him. He drank it black, his muscled forearms resting on the table.

I hardly touched mine, still in shock this was really happening.

The waitress brought our food a second later. Bones had a huge breakfast all to himself with lots of bacon and carbs.

I had a few eggs and a piece of toast.

He started to eat, scarfing everything down.

I glanced around the restaurant, wondering if there was anyone who recognized me. Thankfully, there wasn't.

"Ashamed of me?" he asked, catching on to my movements.

"No." I picked up my fork. "Just ashamed to be seen *with* you."

He grinned before he took another bite. "I used your toothbrush this morning."

"You what?" I blurted.

"Yep." He drank his coffee then set it down.

"Gross."

"I eat your pussy then kiss you and you're fine with that, but sharing a toothbrush is drawing the line?"

He spoke at his normal voice level, so everyone could overhear if they were paying attention.

"Shut up."

He grinned wider. "If it bothers you that much, pick me up a toothbrush."

"I'm not welcoming you into my home."

"Just your bed?"

My eyes narrowed.

He took another bite, still wearing that arrogant grin. "Let's stop pretending this isn't consensual. You went out last night, hit a few bars, and went home alone. A woman like you doesn't go home alone unless she wants to be alone."

"You're drawing stupid conclusions."

"Or I'm being completely logical. You could have taken home any guy you wanted, but you didn't. You went home and missed me."

"What makes you think I didn't take anyone home?" I countered. "Maybe he already left."

Bones chuckled. "If the guy already left, then that would explain why you were so happy to see me…"

I almost chucked my fork at his head. "Fuck you. You aren't the king of the world."

"Just the king of your—"

"Stop it."

He heeded my warning, still grinning, and then went back to eating. "Alright, baby. You get so sexy when you're mad, it's hard for me to play nice."

I bit into my toast even though I'd lost my appetite. "My brother keeps an eye on me. You better hope he doesn't see us."

"Wouldn't care if he did. Actually, that would be delightful." He drank his coffee again before he returned to eating. "And now that he's got a kid on the way, I'm sure he's got more important things to worry about than his sister."

He really did know everything. "Doesn't matter how many kids he has. He'd die for me. And I'd die for him."

"Cute," he said sarcastically. "And I may just end up killing both of you."

"Can we not talk about stuff like that right now?" I asked, lowering my gaze to my food. Christmas was just a few days away, and I would spend it with my family, trying to pretend everything was perfectly normal.

Bones didn't say anything else as he ate in silence.

The silence was so damn nice. I preferred him when we were fucking. The sex was good, and he didn't talk. If he did talk, he said things I liked to listen to. But when the hormones were gone, he reminded me of how vile he was.

And the fact that I had to kill him.

"Where were you?" I asked in an attempt to make conversation.

"Why? Miss me?"

"If I just say yes, will you answer the question?" I asked sarcastically.

"No. You already proved how much you missed me last night." He wiped his plate clean, his eggs, bacon, and pancakes long gone. "I had a hit in Switzerland. It's been taken care of."

"A hit?" I asked.

"That's what I do for a living—kill people."

"You're an assassin?" I asked coldly.

"I wouldn't call myself that." He kept one hand on his mug, comfortable talking about this sort of thing in a crowded restaurant. "A hitman is a better description. People commission me to do their dirty work."

"And you just kill people?" I said harshly. "Without a single thought to who they are."

"You really shouldn't judge me, baby."

"Too late," I snapped. "That's disgusting and wrong."

"Then you must think your uncle is disgusting and wrong."

I lost my confidence, shaken by what he said.

He knew he'd successfully planted some doubt. "It's how I survive, and I'm not ashamed of it."

"You should be. And my uncle would never do that."

"Maybe not now, but he did when he was your age. He worked for the Skull Kings. He was a Skull King. And he murdered all kinds of people."

Uncle Cane was a good man who had been another

father to me. He was affectionate, kind, and never showed a hint of violence. "No, he didn't."

"Don't believe me?" he asked. "Ask him."

"I don't need to."

He grinned. "Because you know I'm right."

"That's not why."

"Yes, baby. It is."

I stared into my mug, feeling my heart beat so fast. I knew my parents had criminal ties, but they wouldn't kill people for money.

"And your brother and cousin aren't as honorable as you think they are. They go to the Underground where women are for sale and they—"

"Don't. Talk. About. My. Family." I grabbed the butter knife even though there was very little I could do with it. "I have every right to hate your father, but I've never said a bad thing about him. You told me about your mother, but I've been nothing but respectful toward her memory. My family is every-thing to me, and I don't give a damn who you are, don't speak of them that way. I'll stab this knife in your neck right now if that gets you to shut up."

He crossed his arms over his chest, his eyes full of intensity. He didn't smile like he usually did when I stood up to him. My words seemed to actually mean something to him this time. "I wasn't speaking badly about them. Believe it or not, I'm actually relaying facts to you."

I slammed the knife down, right into the center of his forearm.

Like he'd anticipated it, he moved out of the way just in time.

The knife was stuck in the wood because it pierced it so deep.

People glanced at us from their tables, hearing the loud sound. After a few seconds of silence, they looked away.

Bones yanked the knife out of the table and put it to the side. "I'm gonna let that one go this time. But pull something like that again, and I'll do the exact same thing back to you. So if you make a move, you better kill me."

I stared him down with the same cold expression he gave me. "Oh, I will."

WE RETURNED TO THE APARTMENT, but I just wanted him to leave.

"Go." I pulled off my jacket and hung it by the door. I yanked off my gloves next and stepped into my living room. "I'm sure you have someone else to kill."

He hung his jacket by the door next to mine, like he wasn't planning on leaving anytime soon. "There's always someone to kill, but I work too much as it is." He walked to my easel by the window and admired the painting I was working on. I was recreating a picture my family took last year at Christmas. We were gathered around the grand dining table, a large roasted turkey in the middle along with the rest of the feast. Red candles were all around, and everyone I knew and loved was gathered together. It was difficult to paint because there was a lot of detail in the piece.

Our conversation at breakfast was horrid, and I had no interest in continuing it. If he said anything, I'd grab that kitchen knife out of my fridge and go for it.

He stared at the unfinished painting and the actual photograph sitting in the corner. He stood with his back to me for a long time, admiring it quietly.

I waited for him to unleash an insult, to bully my family or my artistic skills.

But an insult never came. "You made this?"

I looked up from my spot on the couch, my arms crossed over my chest. "Yes. I'm painting it for my family for Christmas. Since I'm broke, I try to make them things. Maybe when I start making money in a few years I'll actually start buying them nice things."

"Why would they want you to buy them something when this is priceless?"

He sounded serious, but I wasn't sure if he was being sincere. Anytime the subject of my family came up, he was harsh and rude. Seeing my happy family gathered around for the holiday would just infuriate him more. "I can't tell if you're joking…"

He turned around, showing me his dead serious expression.

Okay, maybe he was being serious.

"It's amazing, Vanessa." He hardly ever said my first name. It was usually baby. I'd gotten so used to the nickname that my real name sounded strange coming from his lips. He picked up the painting from the easel then carried it to the couch. He sat beside me as he examined it. The light from the window flooded the room, giving light to the piece. "So much detail. And their faces...look so lifelike. It's only halfway finished, and it already looks like a masterpiece."

Bones always said things I didn't want to hear, so it was unlike him to flatter me just because. He could have not said anything about the painting at all and just sat down. But he seemed genuinely invested in what he was looking at.

I shouldn't care about his opinion, but it meant a lot to me. "Thanks..."

"You don't need to go to school. You *are* a painter."

"I don't know about that..."

"I do." He stared at it longer then looked at the picture in the corner. "It looks just like the photograph. Was that last year?"

"Yeah."

"Your parents didn't buy your other paintings out of pity. They did it because you're fucking talented."

I lowered my gaze, unable to meet his look for the first time.

"Baby, I'm being honest." He carried the painting

back to the easel. He looked at it for another moment before he turned back to me. "Do you have any others?"

"I have one that I finished during the semester. It's the one I told you about."

"Can I see it?"

He just told me he liked my painting, but I was still nervous to show him my next one. I wasn't a shy woman who let people's opinions affect my life. I didn't care what anyone thought of me, only what I thought of myself. "Sure…" I retrieved it from the closet and handed it over.

He examined it with the same interest as the previous one. He set it on his knees and gripped it with his hands, looking at my parents standing in the vine-yards with the three-story villa in the background. It was a stunning picture of Tuscany, the wonderful place where I spent my childhood. I'd intended to sell this piece, but I liked it so much that I might keep it for myself. My parents were role models to me, had done so much for me. One day, they would be gone, but I would have this memory of them forever.

"I like this one too."

I sat beside him on the couch, staring at his chiseled forearms as he held the canvas. It must annoy him to stare at an image of my parents, the people who survived the blood war and lived happily ever after. But he didn't show it this time. "Thanks…"

"What else do you paint?" He set it down and leaned it against the table.

"It's usually people on landscapes. Only Italy, since I've never been anywhere else. But the people of this country love and appreciate their land. Maybe I'll travel around the country and paint different places every summer, like Lake Como, Siena, and other places that people adore. And then I can put them in my gallery and hope someone buys them."

"Someone will buy them," he said. "And I think that's a great idea. Why don't you open this gallery now?"

"I don't have the money, for starters. And two, I don't have any paintings to sell."

"You have this one." He nodded to the paintings on the ground. "That painting could clear twenty thousand euros."

I laughed hard because the sum was ridiculous.

He kept a straight face, staring me down coldly. "I'm

being serious. People pay good money for art like that. Maybe you can get even more for it."

"I appreciate you being nice to me for a change, but I'm an amateur. I'm not at that level."

His eyes narrowed aggressively. "One of the things I respect about you is your self-worth. You never under-estimate yourself and have warned me not to do it either. You're smart, resourceful, and spunky. You're confident but never arrogant. You stand on that fine line and keep your balance. It's hard for me to listen to you talk about yourself like that because it's out of character for you. And frankly, it makes me respect you less."

Now my eyes narrowed in hostility. "I appreciate that you think my paintings are good, but you aren't an expert. You're a bigger amateur than I am. Art is much more complicated than people think it is."

"I'm a customer, and I'm telling you, I'd pay big money for something like this."

"If you weren't sleeping with me, you wouldn't think twice about my paintings," I countered. "You're blind."

"Maybe," he said. "But if you were standing in that

gallery, beautiful and fiery, people would start pouring in—men and women. It's annoying to hear you make up excuse after excuse instead of just going for it."

"Annoying?" I snapped. "Excuses? I need more training before I break off on my own. Only stupid, arrogant people think they know it all—people like you. And that's their downfall."

"You're wasting your money. There's nothing they're teaching you that you don't already know."

"You wouldn't know."

"Yes." He nodded at the painting. "It's pretty fucking clear. Drop out and save your money. Use that cash to open a gallery."

I was embarrassed to say this next part, but I couldn't lie about the truth. "My father pays for my education…" He paid for this apartment and all my food. I was dependent on him, and I didn't like it.

"Then save him money by leaving. Start painting full time. And start selling it. Sell it on the street if you have to."

"Because that's classy…"

"Doesn't your family have a winery?" he asked. "Why don't you display your artwork there?"

It wasn't a bad idea, especially on the weekends in the summer when the tourists flocked to the wine tastings. But hearing him pressure me into these things made me think of something else. "That plan doesn't work if you kill me and my family. Do you make all your prisoners ambitious? Is that part of your torture?"

He stared forward and looked at the painting on the ground, the muscles near his jaw slightly shifting under the skin as he squared his mouth. His large shoulders shifted forward as he rested his elbows on his knees. His size destroyed the cushion he was sitting on, making it sink just the way he did with my mattress. "There's still the possibility you may kill me first. I know my baby, and I know you won't give up until I'm dead—and I expect nothing less."

———

IT WAS THE STRANGEST THING.

Bones lay on the couch, his full length reaching from top to bottom. His feet even hung over the edge a bit. Just in his boxers, he was mostly naked.

I lay on top of him because there was nowhere else to lie. I was in my panties because that was the only thing he allowed me to put on after he fucked me on my bed. A blanket was pulled over my body to keep me warm, but Bones didn't need the warmth because he was his own furnace.

The TV was on, and we watched it together.

Like a couple.

One hand was propped under his head while the other rested on the small of my back.

I didn't know when he was leaving, but it didn't seem like it was anytime soon.

I had to leave for Tuscany tomorrow. That way, I would be there by Christmas Eve. I should have left sooner, but his unexpected visit caught me off guard. I figured he'd have to get back home or to work, but he continued to linger.

I propped myself up on his chest, my forearms resting against his hard abs, and looked down at him. "I'm leaving tomorrow morning."

He turned his gaze away from the TV and looked at me. "Where are you going?"

I didn't like being questioned, like I was reporting to him. "Home for Christmas."

"Christmas isn't for a few days."

"Well, I want to be there by Christmas Eve."

"You can leave Christmas Eve morning." He turned back to the TV like the conversation was over.

"What just happened here?"

He turned back to me, his bright eyes pretty in comparison to his cruel face.

"You don't tell me what to do. You don't give me permission. That's not how this works."

"You're my prisoner, and I own you," he said simply. "Yes, that's how this works."

"I'm leaving tomorrow morning, and that's the end of the story."

He grinned even though nothing about this was funny. "I like making you mad. It's fun."

I smacked him in the chest, feeling his hard body not even flinch. "Fuck you."

He chuckled even though I hit him pretty hard. "Alright, I'll let you go."

"Let?" I hissed.

"It's so easy…"

I smacked him again.

"When will you be back?"

"I don't know. A few days after Christmas. Do you have plans for the holiday?" It didn't seem like he interacted with anyone on a daily basis. I didn't see him take phone calls or text messages. Richard seemed to be the only person he had.

"My crew and I will go out drinking—our tradition."

"Who's this crew?"

"Some of my buddies. We do business together."

Killing people. "I see…" A part of me pitied him for not having a family to spend the holiday with. Going out and getting drunk seemed terribly depressing. I would go to a big house stuffed with people, and we would drink wine all day and open presents. Even Lars shared the holiday with us, getting more presents than anyone. He was a grandfather to me.

"Don't feel bad for me." He turned back to the TV. "I hate that shit."

He was right. I shouldn't feel bad for him. He wouldn't be alone if he valued real relationships and didn't hang out with murderers. With looks like that, he could have found a nice girl a long time ago, had some kids, and started his own family. "I don't."

"Good."

I could feel his hard dick underneath me. It came out of nowhere, and it seemed like his dick was hard all the time. It didn't matter if we were fighting or if we just screwed fifteen minutes ago. He always seemed ready for the next round. "How is your dick hard like that all the time?"

He grinned like I just paid him a compliment. "If it bothers you, make it go away."

I rolled my eyes.

"My dick really likes you, baby. You're his favorite."

"I'm so flattered…"

He chuckled. "You should be. He's a lot pickier than you realize."

"When you're with other women, you wear a condom, right?" Because if he went bareback with everyone else, I was in for some serious trouble.

"That's a personal question…"

"And I have every right to ask. Wouldn't you want me to use a condom?"

"You won't be sleeping with anyone else."

"Uh, what?" I asked. "You said I could see other men."

"Yeah, you can," he said. "But you won't. No other guy will live up to me, so you'll just be disappointed. And if you do, you'll just think of me the entire time. Trust me."

"I've had good sex before."

He shook his head. "Not like you do with me."

I smacked his chest. "Do you ever get sick of being so fucking cocky?"

"Nope."

I smacked him again.

"I like it when you hit me, so keep it up."

I knew he was being serious because his cock got a little harder, so I stopped. "I really hate you."

"You hate me because I'm right."

He was right. I'd never been with a man who made me come apart like that. I'd never been with a man who took me so confidently. His dick was huge, and while it hurt sometimes, it felt so damn good. He knew how to kiss a woman, how to handle a woman. He made me feel so good that the idea of being with someone else really did seem pointless. I liked handsome and confident men, but even my best partner wouldn't compare to Bones. He gave me the best sex of my life. "You never answered my question."

"Baby, I always wear a condom. I've never fucked a woman skin-to-skin before. Just you."

"What?" I asked in surprise. "Really?"

"Yeah. I've never been with the same woman long enough to justify it. But with you, it's a different story."

That made me feel better. It was unlikely I would catch anything then. "But you don't know if I'm clean."

He chuckled. "Women like you are clean."

"And how do you know?"

"Because you're smart."

"I'm fucking you, aren't I?" I countered.

"And that's the smartest decision you'll ever make."

"It's never been a *decision*." It was kidnapping, plain and simple.

"You're lying on me right now, aren't you? My dick is hard but you like feeling it against your clit. Yes, it's a decision. And you make your choice every single time."

"Have you ever——"

"I'm sick of all this talking." He grabbed me and turned me over, forcing my back against the couch and my head on the armrest. He moved me harshly, treating me like a doll rather than a person. He pulled the front of his boxers down so his cock could come out. Instead of getting my underwear off, he ripped them in half like a caveman. He folded one leg against my body, pinning it to the back of the couch, and then he moved on top of me, his big body pressing me into the cushions. He shoved his cock inside me hard, sliding through my wetness. "Always so fucking wet." He pressed his forehead to mine, the back of my leg against his shoulder. He inserted his arm behind my knee, keeping me spread wide apart so he could fit his fat cock inside.

My body was always wet when he was around, ready to take him at any time. We were fucking around the clock, like newlyweds on their honeymoon. My pussy needed to be prepared to take that big dick at any time. I stopped feeling ashamed because the truth was crystal clear.

He knew it.

I knew it.

One arm wrapped around his neck while my other hand clawed at his back.

He thrust into me hard, dominating me on the couch and fucking me like he hadn't had me in weeks. He panted and grunted, working his body hard to give me all of his cock from the crown to the bottom of his shaft.

I bit my bottom lip and stared at his face, watching the concentrated expression as he examined my reactions.

"You love my cock. Say it." He pushed me harder into the couch, keeping my body still so he could ram me harder.

He was already going to make me come. I could feel it in my belly. I'd never been fucked by this man without feeling completely satisfied when we were finished. I never had to touch myself after he left to reach my climax. He always did the job—and did it well. I didn't need my hand for anything. I just needed him.

When I didn't cooperate, he ground his hips harder, hitting my clit with perfect pressure.

Shit, my legs were starting to shake.

"Say it, baby."

My fingers moved up the back of his neck and into his short hair. My nails clawed at his skin, slipping on his sweat. "I love your cock."

He didn't smile in arrogance, but his eyes intensified in arousal. "I love this cunt. Best fucking pussy I've ever had."

I pulled his head toward mine so I could kiss him. "You're the best I've ever had…"

He moaned against my mouth, his kiss faltering for an instant. Then he kissed me again, this time harder. His fingers wrapped around my neck and he gave it to me good, driving me into a powerful orgasm. "Say it again."

I gripped him tighter as he swept me away in the best climax I've ever had. "You're the best I've ever had."

———

I PACKED my bags and wrapped up the painting that I would be giving to my family for Christmas. I left everything by the doorstep.

Bones stood by the doorway, his hands in his pockets and his shoulders broad in his t-shirt. "You know how to drive in the snow?"

"I'm going to Conway's place first. He'll drive."

"You want me to drop you off?"

I laughed because I thought it was a joke.

"I'm serious."

"If you think I'm letting you anywhere near my family, you really are crazy."

He crossed his arms over his chest. "I've been told that before."

"I'll be fine…not that you care." I grabbed my bags and carried them to the car. Straps were over my shoulders, and I had to use both hands to carry the painting. It would make sense for me to make two trips, but I'd rather get it done in one trip.

Bones snatched the painting out of my hand and took one of my bags. "I got it."

"The last thing I need is for you to carry my stuff."

"I disagree." He grabbed the other bag then took the stairs toward the parking lot. "It would be a shame if you dropped this painting before you had the chance to give it to your family…"

I locked the door to my apartment, even though that seemed pointless now because two of my enemies had broken in without a struggle. I joined Bones at the car in the parking lot, and he already had my things in the trunk and the painting in the backseat. He leaned against the trunk, his arms crossed over his chest. He wore a black hoodie over his dark jeans. The colors contrasted against the blue softness of his eyes. Some of the ink from his tattoos extended past the sleeves of his sweater. A few others reached above the neckline.

I stared at him for a second, at war with myself. A part of me would miss him, miss this psychopath for reasons I couldn't explain. He was a paradox, threatening to kill me and my family, and then carrying my stuff to the car like a nice boyfriend.

He cocked his head slightly, examining me with the same intensity as I was examining him. "You think you can be around them without telling them what's going on?"

"I don't know."

He didn't flinch at my honest response.

"I'm close with my family. It's hard to lie. I never lie."

"Just don't forget their lives are on the line. Your silence keeps this blood war at bay. It would be a terrible way to spoil their Christmas, especially when I know exactly where every single Barsetti will be..." The threat was unmistakable, in his words and his gaze. "All I have to do is rig the property with explosives and watch it crash to the ground while you all sleep."

Now I wouldn't miss him.

"Just something to keep in mind." He rose to his full height and stopped leaning against the trunk of my car. He walked toward me then craned his neck down so he could kiss me.

I wasn't kissing him after that statement. I walked around him and headed to the front seat.

He snatched me by the elbow then pushed me into the car door. His hands pressed against the window on either side of my body, and he pressed his face close to mine, his jaw hard because he was clenching it so tightly. "Kiss me, baby."

I kept my arms against the car, my eyes showing my disdain for him. "No."

"Then you aren't going anywhere."

"I could knee you right in your happy place."

"You wouldn't dare, not when it's your happy place too." He grabbed my hands and pinned them against the car, holding me in place even though I wasn't trying to go anywhere. His strong fingers squeezed my wrists. "You're going to be late."

"Let me go."

"No." He pressed his face closer to mine. "I want something to think about when my hand is wrapped around my dick later. I'm sure you want something to think about when your hand is between your legs tonight." He was the most arrogant man I'd ever met, but everything he said was true.

I would think about him.

I craned my neck to reach his mouth, and I pressed a kiss softly against his lips, feeling the warmth of his mouth the second we touched. Scruff had grown along his jaw because he hadn't shaved since he came to my apartment. He didn't kiss me back right away, letting me kiss him for a moment instead.

Then his mouth moved against mine, keeping the kiss slow and seductive. He gripped my hands with a tight squeeze before he moved his hands to my hips. He pressed me harder into the car, his hands shaking with his passion. His hands showed his aggression, but his kiss remained purposeful and slow.

My arms circled his neck, and I kissed him against my car, our mouths moving hard together and breaking part. His large body kept me warm, his dick hardening in his jeans as he kissed me goodbye. He pressed it harder into me, wanting me to know how I made him feel.

His hand cupped my cheek, and his thumb gently glided across my skin. He kissed me with a gentleness that didn't match his appearance at all. He could surprise me sometimes and show a side of himself that I didn't think existed.

He sucked my bottom lip one more time before he pulled away, keeping his mouth a few inches from mine. He stared at my mouth, like he was thinking of moving in once again. But he kept his distance.

I felt like prey as I stood in front of him, his hands on me and his eyes watching every breath I took.

"I'll be waiting for you when you get back." He kissed the corner of my mouth before he turned away. He walked off without looking back, walking across the parking lot and to the street. Even in a sweater, the muscles of his torso were obvious. He was broad like the wings of a plane and build like a brick house.

I watched him until he turned the corner.

Then I finally got in my car and drove away.

8

Vanessa

CONWAY DROVE THE SUV WITH CARTER IN THE passenger seat.

Sapphire and I sat in the back so we could talk. I hadn't talked to her much over the past two weeks because I'd been busy.

Busy with Bones.

"How's the baby?" I asked. "I know you're only six weeks along, but do you feel differently?"

Sapphire was in a long-sleeved sweater dress with a dark blue scarf. Her diamond ring sparkled anytime she moved her hand. She wasn't just glowing with her pregnancy but also with her happiness. "We went to the doctor the other day and everything is going well. I'm taking vitamins now."

"That's great."

"Conway and I are working on the nursery."

"What about the wedding?"

"Well, I want to get married as soon as possible because I don't want to be huge in my wedding dress, but it's been so cold this winter. Once spring arrives, we'll do something small. I'll only be a few months along by then."

Conway looked at her in the rearview mirror. "A little baby bump will make you look sexier, if you ask me."

Sapphire smiled, a slight tint coming into her cheeks.

Seeing my brother act affectionate with someone was gross, but I shut my mouth and let it go. When I brought my husband around someday, I suspected he'd be just as affectionate with me.

The way Bones was.

Fuck, it was the twentieth time I thought of him since I left.

His come was sitting inside me that very moment.

"What's new with you?" Sapphire asked, changing the subject before Conway could say something else inappropriate.

"Nothing," I said quickly.

"Nothing?" she asked with a laugh. "You're always so busy all the time. I find that hard to believe."

I'd witnessed Bones kill a man in an alleyway, and he held a knife to my throat and almost murdered me in his home. Now I was fucking him all the time. My life wasn't the same, and it was pure chaos. No, I wasn't doing nothing. "I've been painting a lot. School was hectic at the end of the semester. I'm glad it's finally over. I went out to the bars with a few friends once finals were over, but nothing interesting happened."

"Are you seeing anyone?"

Bones popped into my mind, six-three and buck naked. His package lay against his stomach as he waited for me to get on top of him and ride him hard. My neck felt warm, and I hoped the arousal wasn't written all over my face. "No. I've been too busy and haven't met anyone worthwhile."

"You could always be a painter at a nunnery,"

Conway said. "They're always looking for new followers."

I would definitely not fit in at a nunnery. Bones and I were fucking more aggressively than animals. We had the kind of passion and ferocity that I'd only heard about in stories. I'd never had a relationship so intense and volatile. He could threaten my family one moment and then fuck me so hard the next. "I'll pass…"

They wouldn't take me anyway.

———

ON CHRISTMAS EVE, we had hot cocoa around the fire and talked about the wonderful things that had happened over the past year. It always happened after a feast, and we sat near the tree and admired all the ornaments that we'd collected together throughout the years.

My mom was always exceptionally happy around Christmas time. When we were all together, laughing in front of the fire, she lit up brighter than the tree. I always caught my father staring at her, affection in his eyes.

Conway had Sapphire sitting across his lap, his hand moving to her stomach from time to time even though she didn't look pregnant at all. Carter sat with his mom and talked to her about his car business. Uncle Cane drank more wine than anyone else, and usually got particularly loud at the end of the night.

I thought about what Bones had said.

That my uncle used to be a Skull King, a hitman.

I shook the thought away.

I didn't participate in the conversation as much as I usually did because my thoughts were clouded by the recent events in my life. When I saw my entire family gathered around to enjoy the holidays, I realized I could never tell them what was really going on with Bones. I couldn't risk their safety, not when my family had already been through so much.

I had to kill Bones myself. That was the only way out of this.

He knew it was coming, knew I would make my move eventually.

That meant I had to be clever. I only had one shot to take him out. Poisoning seemed like the best option, but that seemed too obvious. I could shoot him again, but this time, I had to shoot him in the skull or the heart. If I hit him anywhere else, it wouldn't stop him.

My father moved from his spot on the other couch and sat beside me. He held a glass of red wine, choosing to drink it at family events instead of the scotch he preferred. I knew he drank it when he was alone in his office because I'd caught him a few times. "Tesoro, how are you?" My father had raised me like a son, pushed me to be strong, smart, and independent. It annoyed me when I was young, but now I was grateful he pushed me as hard as he did. I believed it was much harder to be a woman in a male-dominated world than people realized. My father prepared me for that. If it weren't for him, I never would have escaped Knuckles. And if it weren't for him, I'd be panicking right now.

"Good. How's the winery?"

He didn't answer me, his hazel eyes watching me with quiet intelligence. "You seem distracted."

I wished my father couldn't read me so well. "It was just a long semester, and I've been thinking about my future as an artist...stuff like that."

"Talk to me, tesoro. You know you can tell me anything."

Not anything. Not this. "I've liked going to school, but I've been considering dropping out…"

Instead of getting angry or shouting his disapproval, he just stared at me. "You know the winery is yours if you decide you want to take it. But you're very talented, Vanessa. I don't think you should give up just yet."

That's not what I meant, but I appreciated his words anyway. "That's not what I meant. I was thinking of dropping out of school so I could focus my time painting. I want to start my own gallery, but since classes take up so much of my time, I thought it would be more effective for me to spend time creating something…but then that would mean two years of education down the drain."

It would be easy for my father to get upset because he was the one who paid all the money for my education. Even though he was extremely wealthy, that was still his savings. "If you're asking for my approval, you don't need it. Follow your destiny. No one knows the path better than you do."

"Well…do you think that's a good idea?"

He took a long pause before he answered. "There's no doubt in my mind that you have the talent. Getting an education may help you in some ways, but you already have the foundation of an artist, and that's something that can't be taught. It's something you're born with. But I can't tell you to withdraw from the university or stay. That has to be your decision, and I won't influence you either way."

My father had been hard on Conway and me when we were younger, pushing us to be talented and smart. But he was incredibly caring and understanding. He guided us where we needed to go without directing us. Now that we were adults, he was still involved in our lives, but in a much more distant way. He had faith in both of us to become the people we were supposed to be.

I was extremely lucky.

"So, what do you want to do, tesoro?"

"Well...I would like to focus on my painting." I couldn't believe I was actually listening to what Bones said, but his words had been ingrained in me. He wouldn't say he believed in my work unless he meant it. He was honest, even when I didn't want to hear him speak the truth. "I just have to open a gallery somehow. Milan might be a good place for that."

"I can help you do that."

I knew my father would buy me anything I wanted, not because I was spoiled, but because it was important to my parents that their children have what they needed to be successful. But I didn't want his money. I was twenty-one and shouldn't be using his cash anymore. "No, I'll figure it out."

He kept up his stern stare, his silent authority. He did the same thing Bones did, made moments tense with just his silence. It was a trait powerful men possessed. "Do you have a plan to do that?"

"Sell some paintings and save some money."

"Where will you sell them if you don't have a gallery?"

"Well, I was thinking I could display them at the winery. When people come in for tastings, we could have them up. Maybe people will buy them...maybe they won't."

It was the first time my dad smiled. "That's a great idea."

"Yeah?" I asked. "I don't want to do something you—"

"Your mother will love the idea too. It's perfect."

"Thanks…"

He moved his hand to the center of my back and patted me gently. "I'm proud of you, tesoro. You're going your own way in life. In my experience, successful people do that. They don't follow the herd. They become a leader."

I gripped my glass and gave a slight nod. "I know where I get that from."

"You're a Barsetti," he said. "And Barsettis are powerful."

"I know. And I want you to know that I'll pay you back for my education…eventually."

"Tesoro, I don't want your money."

"I know, but I want to give it to you."

"You don't owe me anything. What I want more than anything is to die knowing you're taken care of. That when my spirit leaves this earth, my daughter has everything she needs. Money means nothing to me. You mean everything."

"Daddy…" I could never put this man in jeopardy, not when his whole life was directed toward taking care of Conway and me. He was the most selfless man I'd ever known. He would do anything for me, and I would do anything for him. "I love you."

He wrapped his arm around my shoulder and kissed my forehead. "I love you too, tesoro." He pulled away and dropped his hand. He took a drink of his wine, shaking off the affection because he wasn't an emotional man. He only seemed to be that way with my brother and me, along with our mother. "So…are you seeing anyone?" He asked the question with dread, like he didn't really want the answer. He never asked about my personal life before. But I was almost twenty-two, and he was probably wondering if I was close to finding a husband. I'd never had a boyfriend before, at least one that he met. Growing up, I didn't have a lot of interactions with boys because my father, brother, and cousin scared them all away. But once I was an adult, my father backed off and stopped protecting me all the time.

Bones popped into my mind, not because I was dating him, but because he was the man in my bed. He was also in my thoughts, constantly. He'd taken over my life, becoming the person I spent most of my time with. He wasn't my boyfriend at all, simply my jailer. I was a prisoner, but the only reason it was bearable was because the sex was unbelievable. "No. Not right now."

My father drank his wine again, his long-sleeved black t-shirt gripping his muscles. Everyone else in the living room was talking to each other and laughter broke out from time to time. "If you meet a man you really like, I'd love to meet him."

I wasn't sure why my father was mentioning this now. It was like he knew something but didn't directly tell me.

"I know I've never been very tolerant of men in your life. I was very protective. But you're an adult woman now, and I don't want you to be afraid to bring a man to the house…if you love him." He didn't make eye contact like he did before, obviously uncomfortable by the topic. And he made it clear he didn't want to meet someone unless they could be my husband someday.

"I've never been in love," I said honestly.

"You will…eventually. I didn't fall in love until I met your mother, and I was almost thirty at the time."

"But Mom was a lot younger, right?"

"Yeah," he answered. "She's four years younger than I am."

"Well, if I ever meet the right guy, I'll bring him around."

He drank his wine again, emptying his glass completely. "I want you to be with a strong man, Vanessa. He doesn't have to be rich, but he needs to be powerful. He needs to protect you with his life and love you even more than I do. If he does those things...he's welcome in this house. And I will shake his hand and gladly give you away when he asks my permission to marry you."

Bones popped into my head again. He was the last person who would ever ask permission. He was the last man I would ever marry. He was nothing but a man that I couldn't shake. So why did I keep thinking about him? "You always taught me to protect myself."

"And I stand by that lesson."

"Well, I don't need a man for that."

He stared at me with his authoritative gaze. "But I do, tesoro. I need that."

I might not live long enough to find Mr. Right. Now that Bones had cast a shadow over me, it destroyed my dating life. It destroyed my life altogether. The only way out of this situation was to kill him. "I actually wanted to ask you if you could give me a gun. After what happened with Knuckles—"

"Of course. How about a Glock? They're small and easy to handle."

"Yeah, that would be good."

"I'll give it to you before you leave. You need me to go over it with you?"

"No, I remember."

"Alright," he said. "I can always move you into a different place. Give you some security detail."

"No, that won't be necessary." Actually, it was necessary for that not to happen.

"Did something happen, tesoro? Are you worried about something in particular?"

"No, not at all." I tried to sound as convincing as possible. "I just realized it was stupid to not have a gun in the house. I thought I didn't need one when Knuckles came in, but I probably could have killed him if I'd just had one. So, it's something I should have."

"I agree."

———

I WENT to bed late that night. We kept eating and drinking, and before I knew it, it was two in the morning.

I went into my childhood bedroom where my queen bed was waiting for me. It had a champagne pink duvet with fluffy pillows and a gray headboard. My furniture was gray too, the subtle colors contrasting against the Mediterranean-style windows.

Conway and Sapphire went into his bedroom down the hall, and the rest of my family stayed in the guest bedrooms around the house. If we didn't have a three-story place, it would be cramped.

I stripped down to a t-shirt and my panties and got into bed. My phone was on the nightstand and I grabbed it, seeing the missed video call. It was a number I didn't recognize.

But I had a hunch about who it was from.

I called the number back, the screen black as the call went through.

Bones answered, his hard jaw still just as stern in the dark. He was in the bed I used to sleep in, shirtless and on his side. His broad shoulders were chiseled and powerful through the screen, and his blue eyes were still bright even when there was barely any light. "Hey, baby."

I lay on my side and propped my phone on a pillow, so I could look at the screen without holding it. "Why do you always call me that?"

"Because you're my baby." His deep voice was raspy, like he'd been asleep when I called.

"Did I wake you?"

"Yes."

"I'll let you go then. I just wondered whose number this was…"

"Don't play dumb." He suddenly turned hostile, falling back into his usual stride. "You knew exactly who it was."

I did, and I didn't pretend otherwise.

"Enjoy your Christmas Eve?" he asked quietly.

"Yeah, I did." If he was sleeping in Lake Garda, then he obviously expected me to uphold my end of the deal. He was seven hours away, so he couldn't do anything with that kind of distance. He really did have me pinned under his thumb. "What did you do?"

"Went to the pub with the guys."

"Who are the guys?"

"Max, Theron, and Shane."

"Do they know about me?"

"Yes." He stared at the screen with the same intensity as he did in real life. His black ink couldn't hide his muscular frame under the designs. In fact, it only heightened it.

"You didn't take a woman home?" I didn't know why I asked the question when I didn't really care. The silence felt empty, and I felt obligated to say something.

"Jealous?"

"Just curious."

"No. But I wouldn't bring her here anyway."

"And where would you take her?"

"In the back of my truck. At a hotel. Against the wall of an alley…the bathroom. Wherever."

"That's romantic…"

"You know better than anyone that I'm not a romantic guy."

"And did you screw a woman in the bathroom tonight?"

A slow grin crept into his lips. "You are jealous. You hate me, but you want me all to yourself. If it makes you feel any better, I feel exactly the same way. I get hard thinking about killing you, but I also want to carry your shit to the car and make sure you make it through the snow just fine. It's stupid."

"Yes…it is stupid."

Minutes of silence passed, and we stared at each other through the screen. One hand was underneath my pillow while the other rested on my waistline. My body was covered with the shirt and the sheets, so he couldn't see my bare skin.

He broke the silence with his husky words. "So fucking beautiful."

I kept my face stoic, but my chest rose with the deep breath I took. We were hundreds of miles apart, but I could feel his presence in the room. I could feel his possession through his voice, feel the sincerity in his masculine tone. I could feel his lips on my body even though he wasn't really there. I could feel his big hands brush against my skin before he gripped me. He claimed me without being in the room, claimed me from hundreds of miles away. That was the kind of power he had. "What's your real name?"

His expression didn't change as he stared me down. "Bones is my name."

"No, it's not."

"It's my middle name—and it's the name I go by."

"Tell me."

His crystal-blue eyes didn't blink. "Why? Why does it matter?"

"Because I want to know. I don't want to call you by that name anymore. You call me baby. I want to call you something else."

"I don't call you baby because I don't like Vanessa. You have a beautiful name."

"Why won't you tell me?" I countered.

He didn't answer.

"Why won't you tell me?" I repeated.

He stared at me like he was considering it. Then he picked up the phone and held it to his face. "Good night, baby." He hit the button and hung up on me.

———

CHRISTMAS WAS WONDERFUL, like always.

We had great food, wine, and so many presents.

I grabbed my wrapped-up painting and then gave it to my mom. "This is for both of you."

She smiled at my father before she ripped it open.

Uncle Cane and Aunt Adelina sat next to the fire, his arm wrapped around her while they both held glasses of wine. Sapphire wore the new diamond necklace Conway gave her for Christmas. Carter was sitting with his maternal grandparents and his sister, Carmen. Lars was sitting in his favorite armchair by the fire, still strong despite his age and full of life. Everyone was quiet as they watched my parents open it.

My mom ripped off the wrapping then stared at the painting. Several heartbeats passed, and all she did was look. My father stared at it with the same focus, looking at the group photo we took at the dining table last year. Lars was the one taking the picture, but I painted him in anyway.

Mom's eyes started to water. "Sweetheart...it's..."

"Beautiful," my father finished. "Perfect."

"Amazing," my mother added. "So much detail."

Mom looked at me next, her eyes filled with a thin film of moisture. "My baby girl...so talented." She handed the picture to my father then extended her arms, beckoning me to her.

I left the couch then moved into her lap, letting her circle her arms around me.

She kissed me on the forehead twice and squeezed me. "Thank you so much, sweetheart."

My father wrapped his arms around both of us. "That was very nice, Tesoro."

"You're welcome," I whispered, surrounded by my family's love.

"You're so talented," my mother said. "We're both very proud."

Maybe Bones was right. Maybe I really did have a special talent. Maybe I could create paintings that made people feel something. My parents were moved by that painting, just as much as he'd been moved.

Silence passed for several minutes before my mother finally released me.

Conway sighed. "I give them a grandchild, but Vanessa is still their favorite…"

"Leave her alone," Sapphire said. "That was really sweet."

"I got my dad that nice gun holster," Conway argued.

"Well, a gun holster isn't as touching as a painting," Uncle Cane said. "Vanessa's gift kicks our asses."

Aunt Adelina swatted him on the knee. "Don't talk like that."

"What?" Uncle Cane asked. "Everyone here is an adult—except the little one inside Sapphire."

My mother picked up the painting and carried it to the wall. There was already a picture there, something that had been hanging there since I was young.

It was a painting of water lilies in a pond. She quickly removed it because it was the same size and replaced it with mine. "There…that's perfect."

"What are you going to do with the old one?" Carter asked.

Mom shrugged. "Throw it away. It's trash compared to this."

"Uh," Conway said. "That's a Monet…"

"Whatever," Mom said. "Doesn't compare to an original Barsetti."

9

Bones

I SAT AT MY DESK IN FRONT OF THE ROARING FIRE, enjoying a large decanter of scotch while the snow fell outside. It was Christmas Day, and I spent all afternoon pretending it was just another day.

But no amount of pretending could change reality.

This was how I spent all my holidays—alone.

Vanessa was with her family, drinking and having a merry time.

I might be doing the same thing—if my parents were alive. If I had a chance to have siblings. Their happiness should be my happiness. I shouldn't be nursing my regret with booze. Sometimes it made me so spiteful I wanted to go over there and kill them all.

Including Vanessa.

But I kept my distance and tried not to think about their joy.

Vanessa kept asking what my real name was, but I didn't see why it mattered. I was Bones, plain and simple. No one called me by any other name. My passports didn't even have my real name either because I traveled under different aliases. It was easy to remain above the law when you weren't really a person.

The sun set, and the night deepened, but I stayed in my office.

Thinking about my last Christmas with my mother.

She went to work on Christmas Eve, picking up a client from the street. Money was tight that month, and we were being evicted. She had to find the money somewhere—and she wanted to get me a toy for Christmas.

So she met a client that ended up killing her and leaving her in a dumpster.

My mother never came home.

It wasn't until three days later that the landlord came

for his money. He discovered me, called the cops, and that's when they found her body in the dumpster. I was sent to the orphanage.

No one could judge me for hating this stupid holiday.

No one could judge me for hating Vanessa.

I should just fucking kill her.

Slit her throat and be done with it. I should put her body in a dumpster just the way my mother was tossed aside.

But I knew I never would, no matter how angry I was. I was far too obsessed with her, far too infatuated with her. When she wasn't with me, I thought about her. Now I counted down the days until she returned. When I fucked her, I didn't think about the horrible shit in my life.

I just felt good.

She was like drugs and booze—but with a better high.

My phone rang, and I immediately looked at it in the hope it was her. But it was Max. "Yeah?"

"Caught you at a bad time?"

"It's Christmas—so yes."

His past was just as dark as mine, so he didn't question it. "I think I might have a lead on the guy who killed your mom."

I sat forward, my elbows moving to the desk. "Yeah?"

"I think it may have been Joe Pedretti. My sources say he has a thing for prostitutes—and he kills a lot of them. He was in the area the night your mother died. I can't confirm it with complete certainty, but there's a good chance it was him. I'll look into it more."

"That name sounds familiar."

"Yes…because he's the leader of the Tyrants. They do business with the Russians, transferring weapons and drugs back and forth across Europe. I hate to say it, Bones, but he's pretty untouchable."

"No one is untouchable—not for me."

"He's got at least a hundred men working for him—all heavily trained. He's got lots of money. He has a relationship with the cops just like you do. He's not as big as the Italian mob or the Skull Kings, but he's not a guy you should piss off."

"I don't give a shit. If he killed her, he'll pay for it."

"Let me confirm it before you do anything stupid, alright? And even if he did do it, you still shouldn't do anything stupid. You're only putting yourself at risk and the other guys on the line. Your mother is dead, plain and simple. She's not coming back, the cops don't care, and there's nothing you can do about it. Your mother wouldn't want you to die for her when she's already dead."

Everything he said made complete sense, but it didn't change my mind. "She's family, Max. I don't care if she was just a prostitute. She was my mother and did the best she could to take care of me. Now I'll take care of her."

He sighed over the phone. "Bones, maybe I shouldn't have told you."

"No. I needed to know. You don't have to be involved."

"I'm already involved. I've got your back—you've got mine."

Because we were blood brothers.

"Just take some time to think about it. You'll realize it's pointless." He hung up.

I set the phone down and balled my hands into fists.

Rage pounded in my temple and my heart. The man who screwed my mother and then slit her throat was walking free. I had to dump his body into a dumpster just the way he did for her. Little did he know, he picked the wrong woman to fuck with. Little did he know, her little boy would grow up to be the foulest monster in the world.

Little did he know, I was much worse than my father ever was.

And he would pay for what he did.

I grabbed the decanter of scotch and threw it against the wall, listening to it shatter into a thousand small shards. Richard didn't come running in because he was used to these outbursts of rage.

I snatched my phone and called Vanessa.

It was midnight, so she might be in bed by now.

She answered. "Hello?"

I didn't say anything, keeping my silence over the line.

She knew I was still there. "Something wrong?"

So many things were wrong, but I didn't think I could tell her. "When will you be home?" I needed to sheathe my anger, and the best way to do that was to be buried between her legs.

"Late tomorrow night."

I could make it one more day. "I'll be waiting for you."

Now she turned quiet.

I didn't ask how her Christmas was because I didn't care. I didn't ask her anything because I didn't want to talk. I just wanted to sit on the line with her, listen to her breathe while she lay in the beautiful mansion her father had bought for his family.

"I gave the painting to my parents… My mother cried."

I remembered the painting like I was still looking at it. I remembered the details, the joy. The sense of family was overwhelming, the feeling of friendship and loyalty. She expressed so much in that picture, so much that I never had.

"My father really liked it too. They hung it up on the wall right then and there."

I wanted to say something nice, but I couldn't bring myself to do it. She had the life I wanted, and I was the one sitting alone in my office, thinking about the man I wanted to kill, thinking about my mother's dead body eaten by cockroaches in the dumpster.

Life wasn't fair, and I never got used to it.

She had everything.

I lost everything.

I hated her.

But I swallowed my anger as much as I could and kept my fury bottled inside. I was the one who called her, after all. "That's nice." That was the best I could do, so I hung up and turned off my phone so she couldn't call me back.

I had an endless supply of scotch, so I opened another bottle and poured a glass.

And I drank until I passed out.

———

I SAT on the couch in the darkness of her apartment and waited for the sound of her approach. She said she would be back this evening, and I made the two-hour drive so I could be there when she walked in the door. Her happiness infuriated me, and the only way

I could numb the pain was by burrowing myself between her legs.

It was the only form of revenge I could have.

The only thing that could stop me from thinking these bad thoughts.

Voices came louder as people approached.

"You don't need to carry my stuff, Con." Vanessa's beautiful voice came through the door.

"I know I act like I hate you, but I don't. Let me carry your shit." Conway's deep voice came next. His appearance came into my mind. I remembered how he looked at the Underground, in his finest suit. I'd wondered if he knew who I was—like I knew who he was.

The keys moved in the door.

I was tempted to stay put, to let him look at me when he walked inside. He wouldn't be armed, and his pregnant fiancée would be in the car downstairs. I could kill him then go after her next. Carter would probably be there, but I could handle him if it was one-on-one. Vanessa would come after me with everything she had.

I'd have to kill her too.

But I wouldn't break my word to Vanessa. She kept her end of the deal and didn't tell her family what was going on. So I walked into her bedroom and hid out of sight.

They stepped inside seconds later.

Conway was in a black jacket and jeans, looking so much like his father it seemed like Crow Barsetti was in the house. "You want me to put these in your bedroom?" He had her two bags in each hand.

"No." Her answer flew out fast, an instinctive reaction. She knew I was in the bedroom even if she couldn't see me. She probably felt my presence, felt my possessiveness even in a different room. "I got it. You should get going. It's been a long day."

"So fucking stubborn." He dropped her bags on the floor. "You'd think I would get used to it, but I never do."

"You're more stubborn than I am."

"But much better looking."

I listened to their sibling-bickering with annoyance. I

didn't have a brother or a sister. Neither of my parents lived long enough for the luxury.

"Thanks for giving me a ride home," Vanessa said. "Christmas was nice."

"It was," he said in agreement. "Mom and Dad really liked that painting."

"Yeah…" Her voice softened. "Seems like they did."

I turned the corner and watched them by the front door.

Conway wrapped his arms around her shoulders and hugged her. "Let me know if you need anything. I'm right down the road."

"I know." She hugged him back.

"Merry Christmas, sis." He kissed her forehead then walked out.

She watched him leave before she shut the door behind him. She turned the lock and kept her position in the entryway, her back rising and falling hard. She knew I was just down the hall, and getting her brother out of there as quickly as possible was her goal. She didn't want us breathing the same air. Her forehead rested against the door for a few seconds before she stepped back.

I stepped out of her bedroom and made my way down the hallway and into the living room. She didn't turn back to me, already knowing I was there before she heard my footsteps. Like she was using her body as a shield between me and the exit, she didn't move. She was scared. I could see it in the way she held herself.

It was the first time I'd ever seen her that way.

I stopped behind her, my chest pressing into her back. My arms circled her petite waist, feeling the thick jacket that covered her body. My head angled down, and I kissed her on the neck, feeling her frantic pulse right against my lips. Her heart was beating so fast, the terror ripping through her in waves.

She kept her body in front of the door as long as possible, as if giving her family enough time to get to the car and drive away. All I had to do was pick her up and move her, but she would probably fight me to the death.

But I wasn't interested in them—only her. "You kept your end of the deal. I'll keep mine."

The breath left her lungs slowly, her relief visibly washing through her.

I was almost touched by the gesture, moved by how much she cared for her family. She acted as a human shield to keep me away from them, and the only time she showed fear was when she was scared for someone else.

I pulled her jacket off her body then hung it up by the door. She was in a long-sleeved black t-shirt, and it hugged her body in all the right ways. It showed the deep curve in her waistline and the perkiness of her tits. Her skin-tight jeans made her ass look like a heart. I pressed my body against hers, wanting her to feel how hard I was for her.

I got off on her fear.

I got off knowing I was the man who scared her the most. I had the power to take away her entire family, and I loved having her pinned underneath my thumb. Power was the kind of booze I couldn't get enough of.

Along with Vanessa Barsetti.

I gripped her hips and slowly turned her around, forcing her to face me. Now that I could see her expression, I could see the fear in her eyes. Vulnerable, afraid, and protective all at the same time, she was in survival mode. She wanted her brother out of there as quickly as possible, to keep him away from the monster hiding in her closet. My hand cupped her cheek, and I held her gaze for minutes, seeing the web of emotions deep in her eyes. It was impossible for her to be strong and sassy for me when she didn't care about her own life. She would lay hers down in an instant to protect her brother. She was loyal, having complete disregard for her own life.

I respected that.

I would do the same for any of the guys in my crew, the closest thing I had to family.

I slowly backed her into the door and moved my hands to her hips. I pressed her into the wood, my body surrounding hers and keeping her pinned so she had nowhere to go. Her family was gone, and she was my prey all over again.

Even though I was twice her size, twice her weight, and ten times her strength, she didn't seem afraid of the monster that I was—just what I was capable of doing. My thumb brushed along her bottom lip, and I studied her like I hadn't seen her in weeks rather than three days. I felt the softness of her mouth, the plumpness of her lips. Her makeup was done, her eyes dark and smoky, and her painted lips made them look even more appealing. She curled her hair and had it done nicely. When she perfected her appearance, she was even more stunning. She could be a model if she wanted. She could be the wife of the richest man in the world—the ultimate trophy wife. She could be anything she wanted.

But she was mine.

I owned this woman from head to toe. I claimed her deeply and passionately. No other man could have her because I sprayed my presence everywhere, from her home, to her bed, and in between her legs. "Miss me?"

"No," she whispered. "And yes."

My hand brushed her hair behind her shoulder, revealing her slender neck. "I missed you every night and every morning." I could have gone out and picked up another woman who was depressed over the holiday season, but she would have been a disappointment. I would have pictured Vanessa underneath me, and it would have been difficult because of the condom wrapped around my dick. I'd rather have Vanessa's bare pussy, so wet and slick.

A slight tint moved into her cheeks, understanding exactly what that meant.

"Is that how you missed me?"

She held my gaze, slight defiance in her eyes. She tried to downplay her attraction to me, but every time she did, she looked stupid because it was painfully obvious it was a lie. Last time we fucked, she admitted I was the best she'd ever had. "You know that's the only way I missed you."

I cornered her like an animal, and I liked making her surrender over and over. "I got you something for Christmas."

She kept up her guard, knowing the gift wouldn't be jewelry with a red bow on top.

"Go in the bedroom and put it on." My hand dug into her hair, and I brushed my lips over hers, teasing her.

Her lips parted automatically like I expected.

But I didn't kiss her. I just reminded her how much power I had. I released her and stepped to the side, allowing her to pass.

She gave me a violent look before she headed to the bedroom.

I watched her go then eyed her bags on the floor. I knew Vanessa would try to kill me eventually and spending a few days with her parents gave her the perfect opportunity. While she pulled on the red lingerie I got for her, I looked through her bags.

It was mostly clothes, makeup, and hair supplies. But I found one of her sweaters rolled up, and once I straightened it out, I found the Glock inside.

I couldn't help but smile.

She asked her father for a gun, or she stole one of his. It was the perfect opportunity to get a weapon since I had a tracker in her ankle. I could see everywhere she went, so if she tried to buy a gun, I would know about it.

Too bad I was too smart for her.

I emptied the magazine of all the bullets then put it back as I found it. There was no extra ammunition, so she obviously had it for one use only.

To kill me.

I dropped the bullets into my jacket pocket by the

door then sat on the couch, rubbing my palms together. Vanessa was the kind of woman you should never underestimate. She was getting more acquainted with my power as time went on. She only had more reasons to be scared of me. But that didn't deter her. The only way to save her family without getting them involved in the situation was to kill me.

And she intended to make that happen.

I could be angry, as any normal person would be.

But I wasn't normal.

I was fucking hard.

I loved her fight and her spirit. If she were under torture, she would hold up a lot longer than men twice her size. She had a determination that couldn't be snuffed out, not even by a man like me. That forced me to respect her.

Which was hard to do.

To me, respect wasn't given freely. It was earned.

And she fucking earned it.

She never truly submitted to me. She kept up the battle, silently. She wouldn't stop until she reclaimed her freedom and her safety. She enjoyed fucking me, but she didn't allow that to cloud her judgment. She kept them separate, viewing me as both a man and a monster.

Once I waited long enough, I walked into the bedroom.

She stood up in the red lace panties and the matching push-up bra. She put on the red pumps I gave her, and they fit her petite feet perfectly. Her dark skin looked great against the bold color, the color that reminded me of blood. With her makeup done that way and her lips painted the same color, she looked like the kind of woman you only saw in a fantasy.

My eyes trailed up and down her body, worshiping the gorgeous woman standing before me. Her nipples pressed into her bra, and she shifted her weight because she was provoked by my stare. She wanted me as much as I wanted her, and when she felt my intense expression, it made her feel more desirable.

Exactly how I wanted her to feel.

I stood in front of her, just inches away, and breathed onto her face. I didn't touch her, drawing out the anticipation for as long as possible. I purposely didn't kiss her, saving the best for last. When her lips were on mine, we created a firestorm.

The chemistry was hotter than an open flame. When my cock was inside her, it was like throwing gasoline on top.

And then we exploded.

My fingers wrapped around her neck, and I felt her pulse against my fingertips. It was much slower now that her family was gone and safe, but it still beat hard against her skin. I could feel it reverberate against my fingertips.

I brushed my lips against hers again, dragging them gently across her flesh. I didn't kiss her, but I let our mouths touch. I let the fire stretch between us, listened to the bonfire of chemistry begin to crackle.

Her hand went to my forearm, and she gripped it as I held on to her neck. Her lips were parted slightly, and she breathed onto my lips, her excitement infectious.

I was torturing myself, and I was torturing her.

I wanted to make her want me, to make her beg me. She was just scared a minute ago, but now her desire had bubbled to its full level. She turned into a woman who wanted a man. Our physical relationship seemed to be different from our sinister one. As long as her family was far away from me, she could feel her pussy ache for my cock. She could allow herself to yearn for my kiss.

"On your back." I released her neck, my cock stirring in my jeans because it was anxious to feel that slickness. The longer I made her wait, the wetter she would be. I hadn't even kissed her yet, but I knew her pussy was pooling with moisture. I could excite my woman without even touching her.

She followed my command and moved to the bed. She got on her hands and knees first and crawled up the bed until her head was near the pillows. She turned over and lay down, her knees together and the tips of her heels pointing into the mattress.

I opened her nightstand and pulled out the black leather belts I hid inside.

She immediately eyed them, her face growing suspicious. "What are you doing with those?"

My knees sank into the mattress, and I grabbed both of her hands, choosing not to answer her.

She jerked her hands away. "What are you doing? You aren't tying me up."

"I'm doing whatever the hell I want, baby." I grabbed both of her wrists with a single hand and pinned them over her head. "Because you're mine. I own you. You can fight me the whole way, but we both know how this is going to end."

"I said no." She tried to move from underneath my size, but I was far too heavy for her.

"You think no means anything to me?" I stared at her with ferocity before I took both belts and wrapped them around her arms like snakes. I crossed them above her wrists then attached them to the headboard.

"Stop." She tried to buck me off with her hips. She threw her entire weight into it, doing everything she could to move me.

I locked the belts in place, so now there was nothing she could do even if she got me off her.

"Bones, I mean it." She tried to command me with her expression, but it wouldn't work. It didn't matter how beautiful or how angry she was. Nothing would change what was about to happen. "Untie me now."

I held my body on top of hers, my cock nearly breaking through my zipper because I was so damn hard. She was scared, and she was pissed—a perfect combination. "No."

"Yes." She tried to jerk her body one more time, but it only shook the mattress and didn't affect me at all. "Why do you need to tie me up? I'm willing. I'm here. I put on the lingerie, and I'll fuck you like I always do. Now take them off." A thin film of moisture coated her eyes. Not from sadness but frustration.

"What are you afraid of, baby?"

"I just don't like this. I don't like——"

"Feeling powerless."

When she turned quiet, she confirmed my assumption.

I pressed my forehead to hers. "You will always be powerless with me. So you should just get used to it."

"Please let me go," she whispered. "I'll do anything you want…"

I kissed the shell of her ear then dropped kisses along her jawline toward her mouth. "You need to trust me."

"I'll never trust you," she hissed. "You're the last man in the world I trust."

I grabbed her neck and forced her to look at me head-on. Then I leaned in and kissed her, finally.

She resisted me in the beginning, still trying to buck me off.

I kissed her harder, pulling her deep into me with my kiss. I sucked her bottom lip then gave her some of my tongue, letting it touch hers in an erotic dance. Our mouths broke apart, came together, and then moved again.

Her hostility began to simmer, but it didn't disappear altogether.

I kissed her harder, bringing her into the moment with me. I elicited her desires, made her want me again. I swallowed her fear with desire, made her focus on her arousal and the moisture between her legs.

My hands glided down her body until I found her panties. I pulled them down her long legs as I kissed her, feeling them slide down toward her knees. I broke our kiss so I could move them all the way down. I noticed how perfectly maintained she was down below, which was obviously done for me. If she really didn't care, she wouldn't have bothered. But she kept her pussy in perfect shape for my dick and my mouth. I pulled her panties off and spotted the pool of moisture that had settled into her thong.

And she only had them on for five minutes.

I looked at her, my face triumphant.

She closed her knees because that was the only power she had.

I set the panties aside then undressed. I pulled my shirt over my head and dropped my jeans. My boxers came last, revealing my dark dick and the red tint from all the blood that left my head. I grabbed her panties and wrapped them around my length, smearing her pussy juice all over me.

I moaned as I slathered myself in it, feeling the slickness and the stickiness.

Vanessa watched me, her knees slowly falling apart again.

If she oozed this much into her panties, then her slit must be overflowing.

For me.

The man who wanted to kill her.

Once my cock was covered in her arousal, I tossed her panties aside and moved on top of her.

She took a deep breath when she felt my weight, and

she tugged on the belts, like she might get lucky and they would come free. "Please let me go…" She never begged before, not even for her life when a knife was pressed to her throat. But having her freedom stripped away bothered her on a much deeper level. She was too independent and fiery to be chained down. She was a wild mare, an animal that needed to be free and unsaddled.

But everything would change with me.

I pinned my arms behind her knees and opened her wide apart, the perfect position for her small cunt to take my big dick. I loved taking her deep, getting all of my cock inside her, so she could take every drop when I was finished.

I pressed my crown through her entrance, feeling the squeeze of my girth as I first slid inside. I inched farther in, gently pushing more and more.

She breathed as she felt me, like she forgot just how big I was in the last three days.

I pushed until I was balls-deep, and I held myself on top of her, feeling her slickness surround me completely. I pinned her legs back farther, my face just inches from hers. I loved the desire in her eyes as well as the fear.

She tugged on the belts automatically, like she was trying to touch me rather than get away.

I moaned in her face, feeling like a king who had just conquered a land and took the queen. She forgot how big I was, and I forgot how amazing her pussy was.

How the fuck could I forget?

I started to thrust inside her, to take her perfect pussy with my big dick. I slid through her slickness over and over, all the muscles in my body tightening because every nerve inside me was firing off. Every time I took Vanessa, I took a little more of her. Now I was having all of her, seeing her tied up to the bed and shifting back and forth with my thrusts. Her red pumps were still on, right next to my head.

So fucking good.

She breathed with me, her nipples hard and rising toward the ceiling. She enjoyed it, but not the way she usually did. She normally came within the first few minutes, but now it seemed like she might not at all.

I knew it was because of the belts.

I pressed my forehead to hers and breathed with her, enjoying myself so much that I didn't care about her discomfort. This woman was my prisoner, my slave. I could do whatever I wanted because I owned her.

But I wanted to make her come. I loved watching her give in to her carnal needs, loved watching her give up the fight because my cock felt so good. So I gave her what she needed. I kissed her softly, my lips moving with hers in the way she liked. She liked my hard kisses, but the one she loved most were the soft ones, the kind that were more sensual than aggressive. I kept moving inside her, kissing her like a man kissed the woman he loved.

Fuck, it felt so good.

Her pussy felt even better now. When my mouth was on hers, I got a little stiffer. Our tongues moved together, and my chest tightened in ecstasy. I breathed into her mouth, and she reciprocated. She stopped pulling on the belts and concentrated on me.

It'd been days since I had this pussy, but it felt like months. I wanted to come, to dump my seed inside her and feel it spill out onto the bed. But I restrained myself like every man should, making sure I finished last.

Real men finished last.

Thankfully, her lips started to quiver, and she moved her hips with me, taking my cock faster because she wanted to be pushed into a blinding orgasm. She missed me when we were apart. There was no doubt about that. I expected sex in the morning and at night, and her body did the same—even if her parents were in the same house.

She started to breathe harder, panting as the explosion ruptured between her legs. She came with a whimper, the orgasm so good it sounded like she was crying. She was particularly tight around my dick, flooding me with pussy juice and cream.

"Fuck, baby." I couldn't wait any longer. I wanted to make her come again before I released, but when her cunt felt this good, that wasn't possible. I had the rest of the night to catch up on sex, so I released with a final thrust, stuffing her with as much come as possible. I filled her to the brim, moaning uncontrollably as I hit my trigger.

So damn good.

She finished her orgasm when I finished mine because hers seemed to last a lot longer. Feeling my cock twitch before it released must have fired her up a little more. She looked up into my face with a flushed expression, clearly satisfied by how I just made her feel.

I didn't pull my cock out even though it began to soften. I kept it in there, feeling my come slide past as my size became smaller. I was staying in that same position all night, filling her tight pussy over and over.

Once we were caught up, I'd let her go.

I kissed her again, our tongues moving together as our breath filled each other's mouth. It was the intermission between the pleasure and the beginning of the next orgasm. Less than a few minutes later, I was hard again.

She broke our kiss. "Let me go…"

I thought I finally got her mind off that. "You're a prisoner. Prisoners wear chains."

"A powerful man doesn't need chains," she whispered. "His authority is enough."

I'd said something similar to her when we first met. Now she was throwing it back at me, trying to manipulate me. "Why do you want me to let you go?" I hadn't hurt her. I'd just overridden her, used her.

She held my gaze in silence, like she didn't want to

answer me. She didn't want to admit she hated not having control, even though we both already knew that. Unless there was something else she wasn't sharing with me.

"Why?" I repeated.

"Because...I want to touch you." She spoke with shame written all over her face, and that was how I knew it was sincere. She hated herself for saying it out loud, but she wanted it bad enough to admit the truth.

"Where do you want to touch me?"

Disappointment filled her eyes at the question. "The back of your neck...your shoulders...your chest."

My dick was at full attention, and I started to thrust into her again. "I'm going to tie you up a lot, baby. You should get used to it."

"Why restrict me when I want to feel you? Why stop a woman from fucking you?"

I shoved myself completely inside her and felt my moan vibrate in my neck. "Because I'm the one who does the fucking, baby." I started to thrust into her, and this time, I fucked her a lot harder than last time. I sank her into the mattress and fucked her at full speed, giving it to her so deep and so hard.

And she took it.

———

WHEN I RELEASED the belts from her wrists, she immediately moved away and massaged the irritated parts of her arms. They were chafed in some areas because she had them on for a few hours. She dropped the red bra she was wearing and then grabbed a t-shirt from her drawer. She didn't turn to look at me.

I knew she was pissed at me.

"You aren't sleeping here tonight." She ran her fingers through her hair then looked back at me. "I mean it, Bones."

I lay against her headboard, naked and comfortable. It was almost midnight, and I had no intention of going anywhere. She couldn't make me if she tried. If she went for her gun, she would learn that it was empty.

And then she'd be in deep shit.

I stared at her in silence, telling her I wasn't going anywhere.

"Go," she commanded. "Put your clothes on and leave."

"I'm not deaf," I said quietly. "You can stop repeating yourself."

"Then why aren't you moving?"

"Because I don't give a shit what you want. I'm staying here as long as I wish. Get over it."

"Get over it?" she hissed. She put both hands on her hips, her t-shirt covering her panties because it reached down to her thighs. "No, I won't get over it. I put up with a lot from you, but I don't feel like putting up with you right now." She stormed out of the bedroom and shut the door behind her.

I stayed still, wondering if she would grab the gun and come back. But all I heard was the sound of her making up the couch, getting it ready with a pillow and a blanket so she could sleep somewhere else.

I could just ignore her protest and keep the entire bed for myself.

But I didn't like her defiance.

And a part of me actually felt bad for making her so angry.

I pulled on my boxers then walked into the living room. She was lying in the dark, pulled into a small ball on the couch. She had two blankets on her to stay warm, but that was still nothing compared to my body heat.

She knew I was there, but she kept her eyes closed.

I moved to the floor and leaned back against the couch, my face close to hers. I could hear every single breath she took. I noticed the way her breathing increased, obviously aware of my proximity. "You'll freeze out here."

"I'd rather freeze out here than lie with you."

I stared at her window, the curtains drawn shut. Only the light from the kitchen illuminated the front of her apartment. "You came, so I don't understand why you're so angry. I've done worse things than tie you up. Doesn't make sense for you to get so worked up over that."

"You crossed a line, and you know it. I said no."

"No means nothing to me." I sat on the floor of her apartment, the cold temperature not bothering me in the least. I thrived in the cold. The summer was the time of year I despised most.

"That's a lie."

"You don't know me very well."

"I know you better than you think, Bones. This situation has been difficult for me, and I've cooperated. But I don't want to be tied up again. I hate the way it feels. I hate being restrained. It makes me feel lost."

"Then why did you come?" I countered.

"Because you made me…"

I crossed my arms over my chest.

"Tell me you won't do it again."

"I can't."

"Bones," she said forcefully. "I've made my wishes clear, and you will honor them. This is something I'll fight you over forever."

"Did it ever occur to you that I like it when you fight?" I asked coldly. "That I like it when you suffer? I want you to be scared. It gets me hard, baby. That's the kind of guy I am."

"You're more than that."

I scoffed because her statement was stupid.

"I don't disagree with your statement. I just think you have more potential than that. I don't believe you're as evil as you say you are."

I shook my head. "Then you're dumber than I thought…which is a huge disappointment."

"Bones."

I wouldn't look at her.

"Bones," she repeated, this time with more emphasis.

I sighed before I turned my head to look at her.

She propped herself on her elbow so we could be eye to eye. "I don't like it, and I don't want you to do it anymore. I'm not asking you, I'm telling you." She held my gaze with authority, holding on to whatever power she had left. She stared at me without shaking, making a request that she had no right to make.

Why did I even listen to her? Why did I walk out of the bedroom and join her in the living room? Why was my ass sitting on the floor when she should be the one at my feet? There was something about this woman that forced me to a have a little humanity… something I didn't think I was capable of. "Pick your battles wisely, baby. You've won this fight, but I won't be accommodating for the next one."

Relief shone in her eyes, and she released the breath she was holding. "I shouldn't have to say this but...thank you."

I turned my head forward again. "Why is this so important to you? What am I missing?"

"It just...nothing."

I turned my gaze back to her, holding on to the last word she spoke. "It's not nothing. Tell me."

"If a woman is bound...it feels like rape. But if she's not...then it's consensual. I feel like I don't have any rights or any decision in the matter. Something is being done to me. And it makes me think of what my mother must have gone through...because she never would have stopped fighting..." Moisture coated her eyes instantly, the tears appearing from nowhere. "She must have been tied up and..." She closed her eyes, but the tears escaped from underneath her eyelids and streaked down her face.

I felt like shit.

It was the first time I really felt that way.

It was the first time I felt like I did something wrong.

It was the first time I cared.

That I actually felt something close to guilt and empathy. I couldn't bring myself to apologize, but now I wanted to give her what she wanted. I didn't want her to feel that way, to ever feel like I was doing what my father did to her mother.

I turned my body into the couch and cupped her face. My thumbs brushed away her tears before my fingers glided into her hair, comforting her the only way I knew how. My face moved into hers, and I brushed away the remaining moisture with my lips. "Baby…" I scooted my arms underneath her and carried her into the bedroom where she belonged. Her arms immediately wrapped around my neck, and she pressed her face into my shoulder.

I put her in bed and got her under the covers before I lay beside her. This time, she didn't push me away. She moved into my chest and snuggled with me like she did every other night. She pushed me away just minutes ago, but now she held on to me like she needed me.

My fingers moved through her hair, gently caressing her.

"Why didn't you do it?" she whispered.

I knew what she was asking even though it was ambiguous. When she first became my prisoner, she expected me to rape her. I probably would have if my father had never done it to her mother. It seemed wrong to me, so that was a line I never crossed. I'd kill people and torture them, but forcing a woman against her will seemed wrong, even if it turned me on. My mother was a whore, and men used her for her body. Why would I want to be another asshole like that? I already was an asshole, but that was a different level. "I knew my father did that to your mother...so it felt wrong to do that to you. I have nothing because of what your parents did to my family, but I won't pretend that my father's actions were okay. I wanted to make up for his mistake by not doing it with you...so we're even."

She held her breath after I finished speaking, like she was replaying my words in her mind again. Her fingertips lightly dragged down my chest and stomach, and when she breathed again, she seemed to be back to normal. "Thank you..."

"I didn't do it for you. I just want to right the wrong...that way I have every right to destroy your family." I said the words as I held her, held this

Barsetti in my arms. My fingers stroked her hair, and I lay in bed with her, our naked bodies intertwined together.

"So you won't tie me up again?" She didn't seem surprised that my vendetta was still as alive as ever. But that was probably because she intended to kill me with that gun she brought home.

If she fired that gun, I wasn't sure what I would do in retaliation. I may have to beat her senseless to punish her. Or I may have to kill her. There would need to be some kind of punishment for her ill-advised decision.

I just wasn't sure what it was yet.

"No."

She gripped me harder and moved farther onto my chest. Now she was all over me, treating me like a lover rather than a master. "Promise?"

"I told you men like me don't make promises."

"But you make promises to me…"

I tilted her chin up to look at me, and I kissed her softly on the mouth. "Yes…I promise."

10

Vanessa

I WALKED INTO THE BATHROOM AND FOUND BONES standing at the sink with a towel wrapped around his waist. He was brushing his teeth.

With my toothbrush.

"That is so disgusting."

He kept brushing his teeth, but he wore an arrogant expression in his eyes. He stared at me in the reflection, all the muscles of his body tightening and shifting as he moved around. The muscles in his forearms shifted like piano keys as he scrubbed his teeth. He finished what he was doing then spit in the sink. "I like disgusting."

I slept like a rock last night. While I stayed with my

parents, my sleep was just okay. And it wasn't because I was up late at night with too much wine in my belly. I knew it was because I'd gotten used to sleeping on his warm and hard chest. I felt like a cat that loved to feel his owner's heartbeat underneath his paws. I was scared of this man, but when I was with him, I knew nothing else could ever happen to me.

Knuckles could break into my apartment, but Bones would kill him instantly. He was like a guard dog, a fierce protector. But he could also become the attacker if the setting changed. So I felt safe with this man—but also afraid.

He rinsed off the toothbrush in the sink then dropped it in the cup. "Want me to make breakfast? Or do you want to go out?"

There were so many things wrong with that sentence. "First of all, there's no food in this house. And two, you know how to cook?"

He pulled the towel from around his waist and set it on the hanger, displaying his naked self without any vanity. "I stocked your fridge yesterday. And yes, I know how to cook."

I didn't catch any of that because I was staring at his dick. Even when he was soft, he was big. I didn't know they made men like that until I met him. Some were growers and some were showers...he was definitely a shower.

When I finally lifted my gaze to his face, I saw his cocky grin. "What?"

He walked out of the bathroom, his tight ass full of rock-hard muscle. "I'll whip up something."

I watched him go before I looked at my toothbrush in the cup. I deliberated whether I should take it or not. It was gross that he kept using it, but I needed to brush my teeth. Otherwise, it would drive me crazy all day. The fact that it wasn't that disgusting to me was the most disturbing part.

So I did it.

I brushed my teeth, thinking about my night with him. When I pushed for my beliefs, he folded. He had the capability to listen, to have some kind of empathy if it was presented the right way.

It humanized him, made him less of a monster.

That made me feel like I had some control back, that if I pushed him hard enough, he would give me what I wanted. If something was really important to me, it was important to him. The fact that he admitted his father's actions were wrong told me he wasn't completely evil. He had a lot of darkness inside him, but at least there was a sliver of light.

I walked into the kitchen and saw him cooking eggs and bacon on the stove. "Let me get this straight. You go to the store and pick up all this stuff, but it doesn't cross your mind to pick up a toothbrush?" I joined him at the counter, dressed in a long-sleeved shirt and jeans.

He flipped the bacon, dressed in jeans and a black t-shirt. "Maybe I like sharing a toothbrush with you."

"But I don't like sharing it with *you*."

"If you hate it so much, why do you keep using it?" He turned to me, arrogance in his eyes. "You can get a new one for less than a euro, but you insist on using mine..."

"Hold on, it's not yours."

"You're right," he said. "It's *ours*." He turned off the stove once the bacon and eggs were done. He scooped them onto plates and pulled the bread out of the toaster. I didn't have a dining table because the apartment was too small, so we sat on the floor and ate at the coffee table.

I stopped arguing with him because it wasn't a good utilization of my time. I'd rather focus on eating one of the only home-cooked meals I'd had in this apartment. The eggs were well done, and the bacon was crispy. "This is pretty good."

"Pretty good?" he challenged.

"Alright…" I took another bite. "It's really good."

"That's better." His plate was twice as full as mine, and he had four pieces of toast. I'd never seen him eat anything less than a feast. Like a large horse that needed five thousand calories a day, he scarfed everything down. He ate so much but didn't have an ounce of fat.

"When do you work out? I never see you do anything."

"Because I consider fucking a workout." He drank his coffee, his blue eyes on me.

"And when I'm not around?"

"I have a gym. I do a lot of weights, some cardio. What do you do?"

I laughed and took a big bite of my bacon. "You know I don't do anything."

"Your body says otherwise."

"I walk around Milan a lot, so that must be where I burn the calories."

"You still have a toned look to you."

"I fight off psychopaths pretty often…"

He gave a sinister smile before he popped another piece into his mouth. "You think I'm a psychopath?"

"I *know* you're a psychopath. You kill people for a living, and you want to destroy my family, who are the nicest people in the world. Yes, I think that's the definition of psychopath."

"I've met a lot of psychopaths," he said. "Trust me, I'm not one of them."

"Well, we established last night that I don't trust you."

"But you assume I'll honor my promises."

He had me there.

"You trust my honesty," he said. "So now who's the psychopath?"

I turned my gaze down to my food and kept eating, feeling the tension rise between us. He was a wild animal that could be easily provoked, but I never learned my lesson and stopped initiating his temper. I was too proud and stubborn to be the quiet prisoner who kept their head down until the perfect opportunity presented itself. I was outspoken, and sometimes, a little stupid. "I told my father I'm dropping out of university."

It was the first time Bones took a break from eating his meal. "And what did he say?"

"He said he would support whatever decision I made."

Bones grabbed his mug. "I'm glad you listened to me."

"I didn't listen to you," I argued. "I've just considered what you said."

"Same thing. And believe it or not, I'm a very smart man."

I did believe that. I knew it the second we met.

"What now?"

"I guess I'll start painting full time and try to sell my work. My father said I could put up my artwork at the winery, so when customers come through, they'll see them. Maybe even buy them."

"They'll definitely buy them. My advice as a business man, start high."

"In what way?"

"Pricing. A high price shows your worth. Don't start low and then climb as you earn critical acclaim. Show people you're worth the cost. I'm one of the most expensive hitmen on the market—because I'm the best."

"And you take pride in that?" I asked coldly. "I was walking home, and I witnessed you murder that guy. It's not like you were careful or covered your tracks."

"I don't have to cover my tracks. The police are scared shitless of me. That's what my clients are paying for. When the police investigate the crime scene or they put a detective on the murder, all I have to do is make one phone call and the investigation is dropped." He snapped his fingers. "Like that."

That kind of power just made me despise him more. "No one is above the law."

"Then your entire family would be in prison right now, except your mother. And your father would be in prison for keeping your mother prisoner for months—"

"Don't talk about my family." I didn't raise my voice but mimicked the same kind of authority he showed. I only had a fork in my hand, but I could do some damage with it. My gun was still in my bag, and I hadn't had the opportunity to put it to use.

Bones turned quiet, holding my gaze with his unflinching look. "Then I want to talk about my family. While you were drinking wine and opening presents by the tree, I got a phone call."

I didn't know where this was going, but I hung on every word.

"One of my boys thinks he's identified the man who killed my mother. The guy who hired her for the night, and when he was finished, got off on killing her. Murdering prostitutes is a fetish of his. He's done it to twenty other girls, and he's never been caught because the police don't give a shit about whores—even though they're people. You don't like that I'm above the law? Anyone with money and a little bit of power is above the law. Anyone who doesn't fit into that category is insignificant and isn't even included in the law. That's just how it is, baby."

Sadness sank into my stomach when I pictured how that phone call went. I was having a wonderful time with my family, making memories and imagining what it would be like once Conway's son or daughter was there for our next Christmas. My mother was beaming like a glowing light, and my entire family was happy to be alive in that moment. But Bones was at home, thinking about who fucked his mother and then killed her. An overwhelming sense of remorse came over me, the pain so deep that it ached in my bones. I struggled to accept what happened to my mother when she was young, but she escaped and lived a happy life. She found a way out. She was still alive. But Bones lost his mother...and now he was haunted by the way she met her end. "I'm so sorry..."

Bones stared at me, his blue eyes focused with laser precision. He watched me like he was reading me, and his emotions were difficult to decipher. He was still like a statue, like a gargoyle that haunted the night. "She was killed on Christmas Eve. She went to pick up a client so she could afford our rent and to get me a toy for Christmas. If she hadn't done that, she might still be alive. I wish I could have told her I didn't need a damn toy for the holiday. I wish I wasn't so young. I wish I was the man I am now, the man who could take care of her so she wouldn't have to resort to that dangerous lifestyle." He didn't blink as he stared me down, not showing the sadness that I felt in my heart. All he felt was rage. "When I confirm it was really him, I'll murder him with my bare hands—and leave his body in a dumpster."

I had no doubt that Bones would do whatever was necessary to avenge his mother, and I wouldn't persuade him not to. If it were my mother, I would do the exact same thing. I wouldn't stop until that man got the exact same fate.

Bones was keeping me as his prisoner and threatening my family on a daily basis, but I felt so much empathy for this man. I felt sorry for him, sorry that he experienced so much pain. He was born the son of an evil man he never knew. He didn't have the same opportunities I had. He wasn't loved by his parents the way I was. He didn't have a family at all. He was completely alone…even on Christmas.

No one should be alone on Christmas.

I moved around the table on my knees and got closer to him.

He watched me, his eyes still fierce and hostile. "I don't want your pity. I just want to give you a reality check."

I straddled his hips and moved into his lap, my arms circling his neck and my face moving to the crook between his shoulder and neck. "I'm not giving you my pity. I'm not trying to comfort you. I'm trying to comfort myself…because my heart hurts."

Bones didn't hug me back. He kept his arms by his sides, refusing to be affectionate even though his hands were usually on me all the time. His chest rose and fell at a steady pace, constricting his emotion and keeping everything bottled inside. He pretended none of this mattered, but if it really didn't matter, he wouldn't have mentioned it in the first place. "I thought you hated me."

It was one of the only times when I sat on his lap and I didn't feel his dick get hard. His mind wasn't on sex, which was rare. This conversation obviously disturbed him, emotionally affected him. "I do. But that doesn't mean I don't care, that I don't under-stand. And it doesn't mean I'm not sorry for what happened to you."

After several heartbeats, his arms moved around my waist, and he held me close to him, his arms warm and heavy. He turned his cheek against mine and held me like that, saying nothing.

———————

"WHERE ARE WE GOING?"

Bones drove his truck through the streets of Milan and stopped at a traffic light. "You'll see."

"Why did I need to pack a bag?"

He kept his eyes straight ahead. "You ask a lot of questions."

"Are you surprised?"

The light changed, and Bones drove once more. He headed through the congested streets and past the ancient cathedrals. Despite the cold, it was a beautiful day. The sun was bright, and the clouds were gone. Snow was piled up in the gutters, turning into slush. "I'm surprised you keep asking questions when you never get answers."

"I'd like to know where I'm going and how long I'll be gone."

"You'll always be gone," he countered. "You've been gone since the moment I took you."

I faced forward, abandoning my interrogation. My gun was left in my apartment, hidden in my bedroom until I found the right time to use it. There wasn't any doubt in my mind I could pull the trigger. I may pity him, but it wouldn't change the divide between us.

We were enemies.

We drove for fifteen minutes before Bones pulled into an empty parking lot in front of a building. The property was protected by a thick black gate that automatically opened when his car got close to it.

He pulled into a spot and killed the engine.

What was this place? Did he change his mind about killing me? Was this where he was going to do it? If that were the case, why would he ask me to pack a bag? "Where are we?"

He grabbed my bag out of the backseat and pulled it over his shoulder. "I told you I have a place in Milan. This is it."

I followed him into the deserted lobby and into the elevator. "You're the only tenant?"

"Yes."

Conway had the same kind of set up, but I didn't say that out loud just in case Bones didn't know that. We rode the elevator to the top.

"The top floor is my personal quarters. The other floors are for my…hobbies."

I didn't ask what those hobbies were because I knew it involved violence and murder.

The doors opened to a large living room, designed in a classic Tuscan style. It still had the simplicity his place in Lake Garda had. It was open, comfortable, and beautiful. The living room alone was enormous. He could entertain fifty people, easily. I admired the rug on the floor and the dark furniture. Without knowing the occupant, I would know that a man lived here. "You don't like my apartment anymore?"

"Your apartment is fine. I just needed more room." He pulled the bag off his shoulder and set it on the couch.

Now I was starting to panic. What did he need more room for? What if he had a room already set up with the plastic and the camera? What if he was going to return me to my parents in pieces?

Why didn't I bring that gun?

He must have brought me here so no one would hear my screams.

Fuck.

I quickly looked around for a weapon. There were a few vases and other decorations, but unless I hit his skull just right, it wouldn't do enough damage. I couldn't keep my breathing in check, and my heart was beating out of rhythm.

"Come." He started to head to the hallway. "I'll show you."

I didn't follow, knowing exactly what was waiting for me. Our touching moment yesterday meant nothing to him. I sympathized with his suffering despite what he did to me, and now he wanted to kill me anyway. Maybe my pity was the reason he flipped a switch. Maybe he was starting to pity me in return and he was losing his resolve, so he wanted to kill me now while he could still do it.

When I wasn't behind him, he turned around and looked at me. "I said come."

The elevator was behind me, but the doors were closed. I could sprint and hit the button, but the doors wouldn't open quick enough. Even if I could get to my phone, I probably wouldn't be able to call my father fast enough. And he wouldn't get here for hours anyway.

But I wasn't going to give up.

His eyes narrowed. "Baby, what?"

"Don't fucking baby me." I finally made my move and snatched the large decorative platter sitting on the coffee table. I gripped it with both hands and stepped back, ready to smash it against his skull once he came close enough.

His eyes widened noticeably, like he was genuinely surprised by what was happening.

"If you think I'm stupid enough to just walk in there, you're an idiot. You wanna kill me? I'm not going down without a fight. So bring it, asshole."

Instead of chasing me across the room, he folded his arms across his chest and just stared at me.

Adrenaline was pumping in my veins, and I was ready for any move he made. I had to fight to the death because I had nothing to lose. If I didn't overpower him, I'd be dead anyway.

"I'm not going to kill you."

"Bullshit. Why else would you bring me here?"

"To show you something."

"A video camera and a knife?" I hissed. "Already seen them."

He stepped toward me and raised his hand. "Put the plate down."

"Fuck you." I stepped back as he came closer.

"That was my mother's."

I almost slammed it onto the ground and shattered it just to be spiteful. He wanted to take away my entire family, so why should I give a damn about a plate?

"I didn't bring you here to kill you. I promise."

He said he kept his promises, but he would probably say anything to keep me calm right now. He slowly came toward me, one hand extended. "I have no intention of killing you, baby. But if you break that plate, I might. That's the one thing I have of hers. Make a single scratch, and I'll slit your throat."

I slowly lowered the dish then looked down to stare at it. It was bright blue and decorated with deep sea fish. It was the one thing that didn't match the rest of his place because the color was so vibrant compared to everything else.

When my gaze was lowered, he made his move. He crossed the room and took the plate out of my hand. He could have snapped my neck or punched me in the face, but he walked back to the table and returned the plate where it belonged. "Now, if you're done with your little meltdown, can we move on?"

I stayed rooted to the spot, still afraid of the place he wanted to show me.

"Vanessa, if I were going to kill you, I would tell you. Believe me, I want to see you cry and scream. I get off on that shit. But that's not on the itinerary today." He came back to me, his large arms stiff by his sides as he approached me. He stopped in front of me then looked down, annoyance written all over his face.

"Promise me?" I whispered. Listening to him make a promise was the only way I could really trust him. He said he would always be honest with me, so listening to a promise shouldn't make a difference. And if he was a liar, he wouldn't have a problem making an endless line of promises because he would break every single one of them.

But it made me feel better.

His hands slid up to my face and cupped both of my cheeks. "I promise."

He was the man I was afraid of, but once the danger passed, he somehow became my savior. I shouldn't be grateful for his gentleness, not when he threatened me every day. I shouldn't appreciate his good days when there were so many bad ones. He dropped my expectations so low that every good thing he did was received as a gift. It was a form of psychological warfare.

He kissed me softly on the mouth, his fingers reaching into my hair. He bent his neck down to kiss me and yanked me onto my tiptoes so our mouths could reach each other easier. He pulled me into him and let me balance against his chest, his warm touch surrounding me.

I felt better once I had that kiss, but I shouldn't love his affection so much.

He took his kiss away then walked toward the hallway.

This time, I followed him.

We walked across the hardwood floor and then turned to the door on the left. He grabbed the doorknob but didn't turn it right away. Instead, he looked at me. "I had someone help me with this. If it's not what you want, let me know. I can change it."

My eyes narrowed, having no idea what he was about to show me. Was it my own bedroom? Why would I care about having my own space, especially when my apartment was just fifteen minutes away?

He opened the door and stepped inside first. He moved to the left, so I could walk in past him.

I stepped inside and stared at the floor-to-ceiling window that had a perfect view of the entire city. So much natural sunlight flooded inside, along with the open skylight at the top. It was a painter's dream.

There were three easels next to the window, all set up with different paint colors, brushes, and other tools. A large table was in the center of the room, storing all the extra supplies I needed.

Two large couches were centered around a coffee table in the corner, a place where I could sit when I wasn't painting.

I stared at everything, completely dumbfounded by the sight in front of me.

He did all this for me?

Bones studied my face, watching every little reaction I gave. "I thought you could do your artwork in here. You said that natural light was the most important component to any picture. In here, you have plenty of it, especially since the sun rises in front of the window. Now that you want to do this full time, you need an office. You'll have plenty of space, and when I'm not around, you can come here and use it whenever you want."

I was still speechless, staring at this kind gift.

From Bones.

Was this really happening?

"I...I don't know what to say." Bones was harsh, cruel, and lethal. He still vowed that he wanted to kill me and get the revenge he deserved. He wasn't kind to me most of the time, and he treated me like a slave rather than a person. But then he did something incredibly thoughtful and generous. It didn't make any sense. "I really don't know what to say."

"You don't have to say anything at all." He moved his hands to his pockets and admired the view outside the window.

I stared at his back, wondering if there was a heart inside that muscled mass after all. Maybe there was more light inside his soul than he let on. Maybe he wasn't just a stone-cold killer but actually a conflicted man suffering from old wounds.

"I have to be honest and tell you this isn't entirely selfless." He turned around again, his black hoodie stretching over the muscles of his shoulders. Even when he stood in a room with vaulted ceilings, he still looked incredibly tall. His muscled mass made him appear large, no matter what he stood next to.

"It's not?" I whispered.

"No." He walked back toward me, his blue eyes returning to their cold look. "I want you to make something for me."

"You want me to paint for you?" I couldn't keep the surprise out of my tone. He seemed impressed by my work, but he wasn't an art collector. The stuff he had in his home had been selected by Richard.

"Yes."

"What do you want me to paint?" Maybe he wanted me to paint a portrait of his mother. He'd seen me draw lifelike versions of my family. It wasn't as good as a photograph, but pretty close.

He came closer to me, standing so close I could feel his breath fall across my lips. His hands went to my arms, his fingertips gliding across my smooth skin. He moved his forehead to mine, his eyes on my lips. "You."

11

Bones

I POSITIONED HER ON MY BED, HER KNEES FOLDED and her weight resting on her ankles. I had her in a lacy black bodysuit, the dark color going with her olive skin perfectly. I wasn't an artist by any means, but I knew exactly what kind of picture I wanted. I grabbed the sheets and yanked them back then arranged them around her. I had her hold on to one piece, letting it cover some of her abdomen so the white sheet would contrast against her skin.

I grabbed the diamond necklace I bought and hooked it around her throat before I added the bracelet. I layered her lingerie and jewelry, adorning her like the queen she already was. Her makeup was done and her hair slightly curly the way I liked. Her lips were painted a deep red, and her eyes were smoky and mysterious.

I used the camera on my phone to get the shot, allowing light from the windows in the background to hit her face at the perfect angle. I captured the natural lines of her body, the way the thin material hugged the steep curve of her back. Her tits were pressed together, but nothing more than her cleavage was visible.

I got the shot—and it was perfect.

I didn't even ask her to pose. I didn't ask her to smile or not smile.

She was just a natural.

Sexy all the time.

I shoved the phone into my pocket then walked back toward the bed. I was still pissed she thought I brought her here to kill her. Under the circumstances, it wasn't a crazy assumption to make, but she couldn't have been further from the truth. But surprising my victims wasn't the way I operated.

I wanted them to know I was coming for them.

But eventually, I would kill her. And I wanted this

painting to remember her, to remember the woman who captured my fascination. It would hang from the wall in my office, so when I drank myself into a stupor, I could stare at this image and think about her. And I could remember the fact that she made it, sealed herself in a priceless work of art.

She pulled the sheets farther up her body even though I'd seen her naked on a daily basis. "I'm not sure about this."

"I am." I'd never given her the option. She would make this painting for me, whether she wanted to or not. Sometimes she got comfortable with her bits of freedom and thought she had more of it.

But she didn't have anything.

"What are you going to do with it?"

"Hang it proudly." We were eye level as I stood beside the bed. When she was raised on the mattress, I could stare at her head-on instead of craning my neck down. Being over a foot taller than her had its frustrations.

"Where?"

"Lake Garda."

"Why?" she whispered. "You already have a picture."

"Because I want you to make me something. And the only thing beautiful enough to hang on my wall is you." I grabbed the sheet and pulled it away, so I could see her flat tummy. She had a cute belly button and flawless skin. Her only imperfection was the scar on her arm where she'd been struck by a bullet.

We had the same scar. I just had it in more places.

She continued to watch me with hesitance in her eyes. "I've never painted myself before. It'll be weird."

"You painted yourself in that Christmas picture."

"But that was different."

"How?"

"Because…it's just in a different context. An image is about the viewer's perception. I painted myself the way my family sees me. If I paint myself the way you see me…" Her voice trailed away, but her meaning was still in the air.

"As a beautiful woman I love to bed?" I asked. "No shame in that. You know you're beautiful, baby."

"I mean…as a prisoner."

That's what made the picture even sexier. "I know you can do it." I grabbed her hips and tugged her toward me, forcing her bottom forward and her shoulders back. I yanked until her back was against the sheets, and her hair was spread out around her. I unclasped the crotch of her bodysuit and revealed her gorgeous pussy. My fingers rubbed her clit gently, moving in a circular motion as I stood over her. My cock was already hard in my jeans after taking her photo, but I knew she needed my touch to get ready for me. It was difficult for my cock to fit inside a woman unless she was soaked, so getting her wet was always necessary. If not, I'd have to break out the lube.

Her breathing filled the quiet room and became louder and louder. She stopped thinking about the painting I asked her to make and started to focus on the way my fingers made her feel. When I slipped two fingers inside her and rubbed her clit with my thumb, she breathed even louder.

When her arousal flooded my fingers, I knew she was ready.

I dropped my pants and boxers and positioned her at the edge of the bed. Her legs spread for me, and I slid my cock inside her, easily getting my length deep. I moved all the way inside until my balls hit her ass.

She released a quiet whimper and pressed her hand to my chest. "Too deep."

I wanted to fuck her as deep as I wanted. If it hurt, I didn't care. If she cried, that would just make me like it more. But the second she told me to stop, I listened. She didn't say it to me often, so when she did, I knew she meant it. If she were anyone else, I probably wouldn't care, but she earned so much of my respect that I couldn't help but listen to her.

I thrust into her slowly, making sure I kept the last few inches out of her body, so I wouldn't hit her cervix again. At this angle, I could get even deeper inside her. She took most of my length anyway, so it would be selfish to ask for more.

I gripped the backs of her legs and thrust into her at a slow pace, treasuring the way she looked on the bed underneath me. Her eyes were a little wet from my initial thrust, and it made her look even prettier.

I liked to see a beautiful woman cry.

She stopped pushing against my chest and started to

tug on my shirt. She lifted it up my stomach, telling me she wanted it off.

I pulled it over my head and tossed it on the bed.

Then her hands were all over me, feeling the muscles of my abs and chest.

I loved it when she touched me. She touched me with desire and eagerness. Her nails lightly dug into me, and her mouth parted slightly, showing those cute teeth. Her pussy became wetter and tighter, and her breaths turned to moans.

"Baby...you have no idea how sexy you look right now." She was perfect underneath me, as much of a queen on her back as when she stood tall. The lace still pushed her tits together, forming a delicious cleavage line. Her tanned limbs contrasted against the black color she wore and with her eye makeup. Her dark hair was spread out across the bed, the brown locks striking against my ivory sheets.

"Not as sexy as you..." She dragged both of her hands down my body and gripped my hips so she could pull herself onto my length harder.

Fuck.

Vanessa was two different women. This version of

her worshiped the ground I walked on and couldn't get enough of me. The sex was so good it erased the war between us. When we used each other's bodies, it brought us closer together. We even liked each other, needed each other. She was under this spell as much as I was.

She told me I was the best she'd ever had.

And she was mine.

I stilled my thrusts and leaned over her, holding my mouth just inches above hers.

Her hands slid up my back and into my hair. She fisted the short strands and breathed in my face, still moaning even though my dick was idle inside her. Her pussy was soaked, covering my dick from crown to balls.

"You think I'm sexy?" I whispered.

"You know I do." She kissed me, giving me a delicate kiss in the corner of my mouth.

"I love being inside you. I never want to not be inside you." I was the kind of lover who rarely talked, but watching and listening to her want me put me in a sensual mood. I was more aroused than usual, pulsing inside her because this pussy was all mine to enjoy.

"Then don't be. Fuck me." She kissed me again, this time sucking my bottom lip. "Fuck me and don't stop."

Jesus Fucking Christ. "Yes, baby. Yes."

———

AFTER I TOOK THAT PICTURE, we never left my bedroom.

I fucked her deep into my mattress, pumping her with more come than I ever did before. It got all over my sheets, but neither one of us seemed to care. We fucked deep into the night, past two in the morning.

I'd never fucked the same woman so many times.

By the time I was finished, I couldn't go anymore.

My dick was broken.

She fell asleep instantly, and I traveled into my living room. I stared at the plate she snatched as a weapon.

Like she could have stopped me with a plate.

The corner of my mouth rose in a smile, and I poured myself a scotch in the kitchen. There wasn't much food here because I didn't come here often. I only passed through. Richard stayed in Lake Garda because that was my primary residence.

I liked to be away from people.

People were shitty.

I sat at the dining table and looked out the window to the city behind. The lights were bright, reminding me of other big cities I'd been to. They all looked the same at night. I drank my poison and sat in my boxers, letting the liquor do its magic.

I could normally sleep after fucking Vanessa, but now I was wide awake.

Thinking about that painting.

I wanted her to make it for me so I would remember her after she was gone. I wanted to remember my conquest, like a notch on my belt, a mark on my bedpost.

But then I felt like shit.

It was sick.

I was making her preserve her own memory, capturing herself in a way she didn't want to be portrayed. Once my enemies were dead, I would have that painting as a trophy, to remember everything I accomplished.

But was it really an accomplishment?

I was hurt when she thought I was going to kill her, but did I have any right to be offended when that's what I wanted to do to her? Didn't that make me hypocritical?

And since I didn't kill her when I was supposed to, would I ever actually do it?

Who knew?

My phone lit up with a text message from Max. *Are you in Milan?*

I texted back. *Yes.* I didn't ask how he knew that.

We need to meet. The usual place?

I didn't want them around Vanessa. *I've got company.*

Barsetti?

Yes.

So you aren't going to kill her?

I dodged the question. *I'll see you tomorrow night. Let's meet at our other place.*

———

I WOKE up later than usual because I was up so late. Vanessa was gone, and I assumed she went into the other room to begin her artwork. I changed into my gym clothes and went to my private gym on the next floor. I did an intense workout before I returned and jumped in the shower.

After I had breakfast, I went in search of Vanessa.

She was exactly where I expected her to be, sitting on a chair at an easel. All the colors were in place, but her image wasn't clear. She spent so much time detailing every little thing in the room, from the texture of the walls, to the light flooding through the windows, to the tiny details of the curtains.

She was a perfectionist.

She didn't turn around when she heard me walk inside. Her brush was still against the canvas, perfecting the outline of her body against the bed.

I walked farther into the room, my eyes glued to her painting. But the second I took my gaze away from her artwork and looked at her, I noticed something.

Her shirt.

It was my shirt.

It was the shirt I'd been wearing when she asked me to take it off. It was the shirt that fell on the ground and lay forgotten while we screwed for the rest of the night. I left it there because I forgot about it, and when I woke up this morning I never picked it up.

And now she was wearing it.

Ten sizes too big, it reached her knees, and the sleeves almost touched her elbows. It didn't show her curves, and it made her look even smaller in comparison. Her legs reached out underneath it, toned and beautiful.

I'd never seen a woman wear my shirt before.

And look so sexy in it.

Time seemed to stand still as I looked at her, unsure how I felt about what I was looking at. She had a bag of her own clothes, so it wasn't like she didn't have anything else to wear. I was always possessive of her, but seeing her in my belongings seemed to change my hold over her.

I felt like I owned her even more.

And she wanted me to own her.

I didn't let my victims humanize themselves. I didn't let myself get attached to them or pity them. I had to kill them, so they were nothing more than livestock. Like a cow that would be taken out to slaughter for meat.

But seeing her in that black t-shirt changed everything.

And I would never look at her the same way again.

———

I PULLED my sweater over my head and then put on my shoes.

Vanessa was sitting on the couch with a blanket over her legs while she watched TV. When she realized I was leaving, she sat up. "Are you going somewhere?"

"I'm meeting the guys."

"Tonight?" she asked in surprise.

"Yeah."

"It's almost eight."

I grabbed my keys and wallet off the counter. "I know. I have a watch."

"Isn't that late?"

I killed people for a living. There was no such thing as late. "I'll be back later." I headed to the door, not in the mood to say goodbye. I was annoyed at myself right now. Seeing her wear my shirt pissed me off. I wasn't angry at her for wearing my clothes. That would be a stupid thing to get upset about. But I hated the way it made me feel.

Vanessa followed me to the door dressed in a purple nightdress. Her hair was down, and her face had been washed. She packed her toothbrush, but I forced her to use mine anyway. "Is everything alright?"

"I have to work."

"You'll be back tonight?" She followed me all the way to the elevator, the small nightgown barely covering her body.

"Yes." I hit the button, and the doors opened.

"That's it?" she asked incredulously. "No other explanation—"

"I'm not your boyfriend." I stared at the pissed look on her face as the doors closed. When she was finally gone from sight, I took a breath. I didn't like the way this woman made me feel. When we were together, I forgot about all the shit in my life. When she wore my shirt, it made me feel like I was connected to her.

I hated that feeling.

So I pushed her away—hurting her on purpose.

I hit the button and rode the elevator to the bottom floor. Then I walked to the bar a few blocks away. It was a dark place with guys who looked the other way when they saw trouble. Women were on poles, their titties hanging out.

I wasn't impressed.

Max was already there, getting a lap dance from a blonde. He grinned like an idiot, entertaining himself until I arrived.

I dropped into the chair across from him. "Get your pussy later."

He chuckled then excused the woman. "Like the pussy you have every night?" He grabbed his beer and took a drink.

I didn't like the way he referred to Vanessa, mentioning the heaven between her legs. That was my pussy—and no other man could talk about it. "She's off-limits. What do you have for me?"

A folder sat on the table, but he didn't push it toward me. He studied me with his brown eyes, his hand gripping his glass. "Off-limits, huh?"

"Yes." I challenged him with my gaze, warning him not to cross the line.

"First, you were going to kill her. Then, you were just keeping her. But now, she's off-limits. The only women who are off-limits are wives and families. So, which one is she? I know she's not family…"

One of the guys in our crew had a wife. Wives were safe from trash talk and our general perverseness. And we also had a protocol. If the wife was ever captured along with the crew member, she took priority. The man could die—as long as she lived. When I said Vanessa was off-limits, that wasn't how I meant it. I just didn't want him to talk about her pussy like he had the right to.

Only I did.

"Do you know anything else about Joe?"

Max let it go, probably because he could feel my rage. "I'm pretty sure it was him. I've gathered enough evidence to prove he was in the neighborhood on the night of the murder. That's an odd coincidence."

"Too much of a coincidence."

"So, I think it was him. But you really should take some time to think about this. If you don't pull it off right, all the Tyrants will be after you. If you really want to kill him, do it without leaving a trace back to you."

"I do that for a living, so it shouldn't be hard."

Max glanced around the bar, making sure there was no one around who was eavesdropping. "You're putting the rest of us at risk here. And none of us believe avenging your mother is worth our lives, our livelihood. I'm sorry you're still angry about it, and I don't blame you for being upset, but you should let it go."

Letting it go was easier said than done. "What if it were your mother?"

He held his silence.

"You wouldn't let it go," I said coldly. "And if you did, what kind of son would you be?"

"And what kind of mother would want her son to risk his life when she's already dead?" he countered.

We stared at each other while the music played overhead. The bass was loud as the women worked the poles in their heels. Most of them were just in thongs, their plump asses firm. The lights were low, and their faces were barely distinguishable. Like the other men here, I enjoyed watching them dance and move.

But now that Vanessa was waiting for me, I didn't find them appealing.

Because Vanessa put these women to shame.

Max ended the silence by pushing the folder toward me. "I've got a hit for you."

"Where?"

"Russia."

I hated going to Russia. It was cold as fuck, even colder than it was here. And it was enormous. It was three times as big as all of Europe combined. "When?"

"Immediately."

That meant I was leaving tonight. "How much?"

"Twenty million."

"Wow. This guy has a big bounty on his head."

"He raped our client's daughter. He's paying extra because he wants you to torture the guy before you kill him."

So it was personal. "Consider it done."

———

WHEN I RETURNED to my place, Vanessa was in bed. She wasn't asleep, but she was playing a game on her phone. Her eyes followed me as I walked inside, and she set the phone on the nightstand. She looked at me but didn't say anything, obviously angry by the way I spoke to her when I left.

I grabbed my bag and tossed my clothes inside.

She couldn't hold her silence anymore, not when she realized what I was doing. "Where are you going?"

"I have a job. I'm leaving for Russia."

"Right now?" she asked incredulously.

"Yes. Right now. I'll be gone for a few days. I'll leave my key, so you can come and go as you please."

She sat up in bed, her hair pulled over one shoulder. She looked sexy making herself at home in my bed, lying on the side of the bed that I usually took. "You're off to kill someone?"

I stuffed the last of my things in the black leather bag and zipped it up. "Yes."

She crossed her arms over her chest, turning judgmental.

"My target raped my client's daughter." I didn't have to explain myself. I didn't have to justify what I was doing. But I wanted her to know that, to know she shouldn't feel bad for my victim.

He deserved to be my victim.

Her arms returned to her sides. "Oh…"

"I expect that painting to be done by the time I get back."

"You can't rush art."

"But I can rush you." I pulled the strap over my shoulder then approached her at the bedside. My guns were on the second floor, away from my living quarters, so Vanessa wouldn't have access to them. I stared at her slender neckline, wanting to sprinkle kisses everywhere before I left, but I knew I should leave. I had a plane to catch. "Don't call me. I won't answer."

"Alright."

I wanted to lean down and kiss her goodbye, but that felt too domesticated. I usually kissed her when I left, but now that I'd seen her in my shirt, everything felt different. It seemed like this was more complicated than just a master and a prisoner.

She stared at me, like she was thinking the same thing.

I finally had the strength to turn away and walk to the door.

"Bones."

I stood at the doorway, still gripping the strap of my bag. I didn't want to turn around, I didn't want to look at her. I just wanted to walk off like she meant nothing to me. But I turned around anyway.

She moved to her knees then pulled the purple night-dress over her head, revealing her gorgeous tits, sexy curves, and beautiful skin. Her dark skin looked good under any light, but right now, it looked especially stunning.

Fucking kissable.

"You're just going to leave without saying goodbye to your baby?"

I never got so hard so fast in my life. My bag dropped to the floor with a thud, and I pulled my shirt over my head. This woman wanted me and was pretty much begging me. My assignment didn't seem important anymore, not when her tits looked that gorgeous and her nipples were so hard. Her little belly was calling to me, asking for my kisses.

I kicked off my shoes then dropped my pants. Bits of clothing dropped on the floor until I reached the bed buck naked.

Vanessa grabbed me by the arm and pulled me on top of her, her legs immediately circling my waist and her fingers running through my hair. Her mouth was on mine, and she kissed me like a woman who didn't want her man to leave.

My cock found her pussy like a magnet, and I slid inside her, greeted by her arousal.

"Apologize to me."

I was so hard inside her, oozing from my crown because I was so turned on. I loved being the master, keeping my prisoner in line. But when she became sassy, needy, it hit the right spot. "I'm sorry, baby."

"Don't ever leave like that again."

"I won't."

She kissed me hard, her hips rocking with mine so she could take my cock hard and fast. "Promise me."

I was sick of making promises. I was tired of making exceptions for her. I was pissed at myself for bending all the rules for her. She was still alive because I allowed it, and I was buried between her legs right this very moment because she made me weak. Our relationship had turned into this combustive explosion of intense chemistry that made both of us stupid and irrational…and made us despise each other more at the same time. I hated her because of what she did to me. And she hated me for making her feel so much shame, for enjoying the feeling of her enemy's cock deep inside her. But I made another promise to her, a promise I would keep because I was a man of my word. "I promise."

12

Vanessa

WHEN I WOKE UP THE NEXT MORNING, THE SHAME hit me.

Hard.

What the fuck was I doing?

I'd always been attracted to Bones, but now I was starting to need him. I wanted all of him all the time. Once I got some of that intensity between us, I didn't want to let go. A man had never made me feel the way he did. I felt so sexy and beautiful, whether I was dressed in lingerie with makeup or lying around in a baggy shirt with a clean face. No man had ever made me feel this kind of addiction, of wanting more and more.

I wasn't sure if I could quit.

Now I had to wonder if I was doing this because I had to…or because I wanted to.

That's when I started to cry.

I wasn't the kind of person who cried. Crying was weak and annoying. My mother never did it, and I wasn't going to start now. But I felt so trapped. I had no one to turn to for help, no one to talk to. I was stuck in this open prison, feeling things for the man who made me his captive.

I liked kissing him.

Touching him.

Fucking him.

And I knew he felt the same way. Bones felt the same disgusting need I did. He wanted to be between my legs every night and not with other women. He hated me for what I'd done to his family, but he didn't kill me because he'd become too attached.

I'd become too attached too.

What would happen if I didn't stop this?

Would I ever be free?

Or would I be the one who wound up dead? I couldn't be the weak one. One of us had to kill the other.

And I wasn't going to let him be the one to pull the trigger.

Only one of us could get out of this alive.

And it was going to be me.

———

DAYS WENT BY, and I stayed at his place. He left me a key and the code to get in and out. I didn't have access to the other floors, and I was curious to know what was there. He worked out, so he must have a gym somewhere. And he killed people, so he must have weapons too. But I didn't find any.

I worked on my painting most of the time, taking advantage of the morning light to get the best colors for the picture. In the beginning, it was strange to paint myself in a sexy way, especially when I knew what happened after this photo was taken.

We fucked nonstop.

But after a few hours, I got over it.

I worked on all the specific details, treating the image as if it were a random person instead of myself. I spent a lot of time working on every single color to make sure it was as realistic as possible. I had to mix the paints and add different concentrations to get the right consistency. Even the smallest touches were a long process because they required so much time and detail.

The days passed, and I kept working, getting so involved in the painting that I became more invested in it than I was at the beginning. I did my best to capture the right tone, to change the colors a little to set the mood. I painted myself exactly the way he saw me, as a beautiful prisoner that he couldn't torture— but couldn't release either.

By the time I was done, I couldn't stop staring at it.

It was beautiful.

It wasn't stunning because of me. It was stunning because it captured that moment in time so perfectly. That was the beauty of a painting versus a regular photograph. So much more could be captured with the colors and the texture. It wasn't identical to the picture, and that was because a picture couldn't capture the mood.

But a painting could.

Anyone could look at this painting and feel exactly what I felt, understand exactly what I felt. There was so much passion and restrained lust. There was so much affection and infatuation. I could feel his eyes on me as I stared at it, remembering exactly how it felt when he stared at me with that brooding gaze.

I didn't just capture my presence in the painting —but his.

I set my brushes down and continued to look at it, imagining it hanging in his office. It was hard to understand why he would want a painting when he already had me. Why spend time looking at it when he could just look at me in the flesh instead. He wasn't an art lover or an artistic person.

So why did he want it?

And then it hit me.

He wanted it because I wouldn't always be around to look at.

Because I would soon be a memory.

And he wanted to remember exactly how it felt to

have me, to have me in his captivity, to feel this balance between passion and hate.

My fingers started to shake, but I forced them to steady. Bones had never misled me about his intentions with me. He enjoyed my body, but he would eventually stop my beating heart. He just had to decide when he was ready to do it, after he was finally tired of me.

Maybe that was sooner than I realized.

There was no time to waste.

The next time he was at my apartment, I would have to pull the trigger.

And kill this monster.

———

I HADN'T SPOKEN to him in four days.

I returned to my place because I didn't want to be near his stuff anymore. I didn't want to paint in that beautiful room because it would only soften my heart. He claimed he only gave me that room so I could make his painting, but I suspected he also did it for me—so his plaything would have something to do.

I took the painting to my apartment because I never intended to give it to him. He would come over when he came back to town, but he wouldn't leave this apartment after he walked in the door.

I'd kill him then call my father.

He'd know what to do with the body. Hopefully, he wouldn't ask too many questions.

I couldn't look my father in the eye and tell him I was sleeping with Bones.

That would be the most uncomfortable conversation of my life.

I wasn't sure what I would do with the painting. It would be strange to keep it because it was an image of myself dressed in lingerie in a man's bed. It would be weird to hang it proudly on the wall. I should probably just burn it.

But it seemed a waste to burn something so beautiful.

Something I put so much time into.

Just because it depicted something dark and twisted didn't make it ugly. It was truthful and honest, transparent in its emotions. Bones had some artistic capability because he was the one who took the photo. I just added the emotion to it.

I placed the gun underneath my pillows where I slept, knowing he would give me no warning before he walked through the front door. He wouldn't tell me he was back in town until he marched into my apartment and announced it.

I had to be ready.

I was sitting in my living room having dinner with the painting on the easel next to the window when I heard footsteps outside my front door. I stopped eating and listened, my heart beating hard in my chest. I knew it was him before I saw him, before I even heard him.

I could just feel him.

He must have picked the lock because it took him a few seconds before he opened the door and welcomed himself inside.

It annoyed me because he knew I was home. All he had to do was knock.

He stepped inside, dressed in all black. His heavy frame thudded against the floor as he moved, and his crystal-blue eyes landed on me once he was inside the living room. He stared at me with various emotions, different intensities. He seemed angry, but he also seemed desperate.

I wasn't nervous because of the way he was staring at me. I was nervous because of what I was about to do.

I knew it was just my paranoia, but it seemed like he knew my plan.

He turned his gaze to the painting and stilled as he stared at it. Then he crossed the room to get a better look at it. His back was to me, and he crossed his arms over his chest.

I stared at his shoulders, watching them rise and fall as he breathed. I wondered what he was thinking, if he loved it or connected with it. Was it exactly what he wanted? Was it the perfect image to remember me by? He was unpredictable, so he could snap it in half at any moment.

Time passed, and he still didn't move. Not a single word was spoken. He kept the same stance as he stared at it, his entire body still with the exception of his breathing. Minutes trickled by until half an hour came and went.

Then a full hour passed.

And he continued to stare.

I went to his side, staring at the same image he was staring at. I took a peek at his face, hoping to grasp his thoughts based on his appearance. But his blue eyes were unreadable, and his jawline was as hard as ever. He wore an expression of constant anger. The only time that ever changed was when he was being a smartass or he was thrusting inside me. Otherwise, he was always this concrete wall.

We still hadn't spoken a word to each other since he walked through the door. He didn't ask why I was there instead of his apartment, and he didn't tell me how his hit in Russia went. He didn't make a smartass comment about missing me. He didn't kiss me either. We seemed to have a conversation without words.

Like being in the same room together was enough for us to communicate.

When other fifteen minutes passed and he kept staring at the painting, there was no doubt he loved it. He wouldn't stare so long unless it made him feel something, stimulated his brain as well as his heart.

He finally turned his head my way, looking at me head-on.

But there still wasn't a single word.

I hated feeling this way. I hated the way my knees got a little weak when he looked at me that way. I hated myself for feeling a little relief knowing he came back from his mission alive. I hated feeling the slight ache in my lips because he hadn't kissed me yet. I hated the way I wanted to go to the bedroom, and not because I wanted to put a bullet in his brain.

How did I feel all this for a man I despised?

What he did to me was unforgivable. I couldn't forget that. I never would.

But human emotion was complicated. My painting alone was proof of that.

He suddenly pulled his sweater over his head, taking the shirt with it. His muscled frame came into view, the cuts and lines of separation in his muscles obvious even when it was dark. With powerful shoulders that could carry the weight of the world and a chest that was harder than concrete, he was built like a tank. He took that bullet without flinching because he was immune to pain. He didn't need a bulletproof vest because a gun couldn't perforate his hard exterior.

He moved into me, his hands cupping my face gently

as his mouth took my kiss. His lips pressed against mine as one hand snaked to the back of my head. He guided me into him, kissing me like it was the first time he ever had the opportunity.

My hands went to his chest, and I kissed him back without thinking twice about my actions. Everything was natural, thoughtless. When I was with this man, I never thought twice about what I was doing. I just felt everything he gave me, felt the way our mouths moved together perfectly. Why did the man I hated most have to be the man I wanted the most? Why couldn't another man kiss me like this? Fuck me as good?

He pulled my shirt over my head and snapped my bra off as he guided me backward to the bedroom.

This was it—now or never.

My nails dug into him, not out of passion, but terror. If I didn't get this right, I didn't know what he would do to me. He still intended to kill me, so he might break my skull with his bare hands.

His palms went to my tits, and he squeezed them as he guided me to the bed. When the backs of my knees hit the mattress, he pinched my nipples gently. My jeans were undone then his came loose.

He pushed me back on the bed before he tugged them off, getting them down to my ankles before he pulled my thong with it. Then he dropped his clothes, bringing out his big cock.

I missed that cock.

Killing him almost seemed like a waste, when he was so gifted in many areas. Men weren't built like this. Men weren't big like this. And men didn't fuck like this. He had so much potential—but it was all wasted.

He moved on top of me, his knees separating mine. His weight sank me into the mattress, and he gave me that possessive expression, the kind that told me I was his the second he walked in that door.

My head lay back on the pillow, and that's when I felt the gun underneath my head.

The shape was distinct through the soft pillows. I could distinguish the barrel from the butt.

This was the perfect time. When he thrust inside me, he was distracted. He was focused on his dick inside me, on the wetness between my legs. And when his lips were on mine, he wasn't aware of anything else around us.

Just us.

He pointed his dick at my entrance and slid inside.

I gripped his arms and moaned, forgetting how good that felt over the last four days.

Damn…so good. I felt so full, so right.

Maybe I should do it tonight. I would never have better sex than this for the rest of my life, so I should just enjoy it while I could.

But no, there may not be another chance.

I shouldn't spare his life just because he was good in bed.

I had to do this.

If I didn't, I would never be free.

My family would never be free.

He thrust into me with even and deep strokes, his mouth moving with mine. He breathed into me as he pumped, giving me his dick at the perfect angle. He played with my mouth, kissing me and teasing me as we moved together. "I missed you, baby."

The words came out of my lips automatically before I could even think enough to stop them. "I missed you too…"

His dick thickened a little more inside me, loving that response. He kept kissing me, moaning with me from time to time.

I touched his body in different places, never keeping my hands in the same spot. I opened my eyes to look into his and saw that they were closed. Despite the terror in my heart, I made my move. I slid my hand under the pillow without breaking my kiss and reached the butt of the gun. I carefully slid it out from underneath me, kissing him a little harder once my head sank a few more inches where the gun had been.

I pointed the gun to the ground and clicked off the safety.

Fuck, I had to do this.

Point it at his head and pull the trigger. Just like that.

And all of this would be over.

I would be free again.

I tried not to think and just raised the gun. I watched myself point the barrel at his temple, keeping it at point blank range without touching his skin.

He spoke into my mouth. "Do it."

My heart nearly leaped up my throat and into my mouth.

He opened his eyes and looked at me, not breaking his stride as he continued to fuck me. He stopped kissing me and never looked at the gun. He must have seen it in his peripheral vision because he never turned toward it. "Come on, baby. Do it." He grabbed my wrist and pressed the barrel right against his temple.

Jesus Christ.

He held his body on top of mine, his cock harder than ever before. It was pulsing inside me, throbbing with imminent explosion. He breathed harder and started to fuck me faster. "This is the only chance you're going to get. So take it."

My hand shook as I held the Glock. It was heavy, but it was even heavier with the weight of death. All I had to do was pull the trigger, and he would collapse on top of me. He wouldn't survive a shot to the head, and if he did, he wouldn't be strong enough to stop me from shooting him again.

"Baby." He kissed me hard on the mouth, breathing into me. "You're stronger than this. I've promised to kill you and your whole family. I've kept you as a prisoner and fucked you every chance I could get. You should kill me. I deserve it."

Everything he said was true, but my finger wouldn't squeeze the trigger. This was my opening, but I didn't take it. I'd killed a man before, so this shouldn't be any different. This was about survival. Just shoot and be done with it.

But my hand shook, and my finger didn't move.

He pressed his forehead to mine and rocked with me, his cock so hard it seemed like he could barely fit inside me. His hand moved into my hair, and he kissed me like there wasn't a gun pointed to his head. He fisted my hair and kept me in place, grinding against me just the way I liked. He gave me his tongue and his passion, gave me everything like he usually did. This man was fearless, not afraid of death or pain. He didn't flinch when I shot him in the shoulder, and he kissed me just the way he did now.

Maybe he did want me to shoot him.

But I couldn't do it.

I hated this man. Truly, I did.

But something steadied my hand.

I set the gun on my nightstand before returning my hand to his arm.

He stopped moving, ending his kiss and everything else. He stared down at me, his expression unreadable. He seemed angry but moved at the same time. His fingers moved in my hair, and his cock was still raging hard. "I couldn't do it either, baby."

———————

WITH THE GUN on the nightstand and the large man still in my bed, I went into the kitchen and made a pot of coffee. I found his t-shirt on the way, so I pulled that over my head and let it touch my knees. Ten sizes too big, it wasn't flattering to my curves at all, but it was the most comfortable piece of clothing I'd ever worn.

Probably because it smelled like him.

I watched the coffee pot work the grinds to produce the caffeinated liquid as I stood at the counter, thinking of last night.

Thinking of the way I put that gun to his head.

But didn't shoot.

I didn't fucking shoot.

He told me to but I didn't. He reminded me of all the reasons why I should. He knew there was a good chance I would actually do it because I'd shot him before—with the intention to kill.

But I turned soft and set the gun down.

Maybe it was because he was in between my legs. Maybe it was because his mouth was mine. Maybe I was too attached to him to actually blow his brains out. I decided this was the only way out of my situation, the only way I could protect myself and my family.

But I didn't do it.

Maybe if he never said anything, I would have pulled the trigger. Maybe if he'd kept kissing me and wasn't aware of the barrel near his skull, I would have talked myself into doing it. But hearing him coach me to do it, feeling his cock get even harder with the threat of violence upon him, just confused me.

And now my chance was gone.

The coffee was done, but I continued to stand there, wearing his t-shirt with the sunlight coming through the window. He was asleep in the other room, the gun still sitting there. I could walk back in there and kill him now.

But I knew I wouldn't.

Footsteps sounded behind me, his weight making the floor creak in certain places. The sound became louder once he entered the kitchen.

I could feel his stare the second he was in the room.

He stopped for a long time, just staring at me.

I didn't turn around. I didn't want to look at him. I didn't want to face the shame of my weakness.

He came behind me and placed his large hands on the backs of my arms. He stood there, breathing down on me like a tiger that just cornered his prey.

I stayed absolutely still, my heart beating in my throat because I was both scared and nervous. After a night like that, I didn't know what would happen between us. I didn't know if he would punish me for the attempt or if he would be disappointed I didn't do it.

He slowly turned me around, forcing me to meet his gaze head-on.

I didn't want to look at his handsome face, to see the arrogance and the possession. I didn't want to see the victory in his eyes. Not only did he keep me as his prisoner, but he had a prisoner that was too weak to kill him.

I never felt more pathetic in my life.

He lifted me onto the kitchen counter and stood between my legs, his strong arms scooping me and holding me against him. My countertops were high, so it brought me to eye level with his gaze.

Gently, he leaned in and kissed me on the mouth, giving me a good morning kiss that was softer than all the others he gave me. Then he rested his forehead against mine, his eyes looking down at my lips.

"I hate you." My hands slid up his arms until they gripped his biceps. "I do…"

"I know, baby."

"I wish that I killed you. I wish I could do it."

"I know that too." He kissed the corner of my mouth.

"I don't know why I didn't…" My eyes shifted down because I was too embarrassed to meet his gaze. I'd never been filled with such self-loathing. If my father knew what I did, he would be disappointed in me. "I was going to kill you and keep that painting. Getting rid of you is the only solution to my problem. I'm ashamed of myself." I closed my eyes, unable to take that icy stare.

His fingers went to my chin, forcing my head up.

I opened my eyes and looked at him again.

"I couldn't do it either, baby."

"Why?" I whispered.

His fingers slid down my neck, right over my pulse. "Seemed like a waste to me. You're so smart, strong, beautiful…so much potential. You have more strength than most men I come across. Every woman should be raised the way you've been raised. Maybe if my mother had more of your qualities, she would still be alive right now."

Anytime he mentioned his mother, I felt a twinge of sadness. It was the one characteristic that humanized him. He loved his mother and never cared that she was a prostitute. Other people would turn their backs on their mother or daughter for resorting to that livelihood, but Bones never judged her for it. It made me respect him.

"Why didn't you kill me?"

I didn't have an answer for that. "I…I don't know." The only way out of this mess was to kill him, and I passed on the opportunity. I should have a stronger reason for letting him live, but I wasn't sure what that reason was. Maybe I thought it was a waste too, that Bones had the potential to be something more. "I think this…" My hands moved to his shoulders, and I squeezed him. "Stops me from thinking clearly. I fall into you, and I don't think about anything else. It's like there's two different versions of us. I despise everything about you, but we have this…I don't even know what it is."

"Passion. Lust. Connection. Affection. Respect…"

"Yeah, I guess."

He pressed his forehead to mine. "I understand that all too well."

"I don't know what to do…" I closed my eyes and held on to him, seeking comfort from my tormentor. He could take me to bed right this second, and I wouldn't fight him. I'd spread my legs and pull him deeper into me. I'd want more than what he could give. "Please leave my family alone. Just drop it, okay?"

He stood in silence, his hands still on my waist.

I opened my eyes and looked at him. "Please."

"You know I can't do that…"

"I could have killed you, but I didn't. You owe me."

He stared at me with his blue eyes, his expression unreadable.

"Bones, hurting my family isn't going to bring yours back. It's not going to rewrite history. You'll just make your life feel more hollow. And you'll only hurt me… I know you don't want to hurt me."

"I do want to hurt you, Vanessa," he whispered. "My intentions toward you have never changed. You still hate me, I still hate you."

"But we both feel something else besides hate toward each other…"

He didn't deny it. "Yes. But we're still on opposite sides of the battlefield. Your family not only destroyed mine but ruined my inheritance. If my mother had what she needed, she wouldn't have been a whore. And I'm sure being a prostitute was just as painful as her eventual death."

"My family was just trying to protect themselves. Surely, you must see it as a retaliation, not a provocation. Your father killed my aunt and raped my mother. You think those crimes don't deserve to be punished?"

He held my gaze, his expression unreadable. "I won't say what he did was right. But your family's actions ruined my life. My mother was innocent. I was innocent. You got to grow up in a family who adored you in a beautiful mansion. You had everything I never did. I will always hate you for that, for having the life that should have been mine."

Tears welled up in my eyes. "I'm sorry that happened to you. I am. What if my family gave you money—"

"I don't want their money. I want my money." He pulled his hands from my hips, his anger starting to flood in his veins. "You don't get it. I'm starting to think you'll never get it."

We were back to where we started, and it made me wonder if we'd grown at all. He held a knife to my throat but didn't kill me. I held a gun to his head but didn't pull the trigger. It seemed like so much had changed, but it never really did. "That painting…did you want me to make it so you could remember me? Because you're going to kill me?"

He held my gaze, his expression as hard as ice. He

said he would never lie to me, that he would always give me his honesty. So whatever answer he gave next was the truth. "Yes."

I took a deep breath, feeling the regret circulate through my heart. "Why didn't I kill you?" I should have pulled the trigger. I should have ended his life last night.

He suddenly walked away, leaving me sitting on the kitchen counter to deal with my feelings.

I didn't shoot him because it felt wrong, but now I wished I had. My life was on the line. He intended to kill me, and even though I didn't put a bullet in his brain, that didn't mean he would be so kind toward me.

He walked back inside with the gun pointed to the ground. He handed it to me.

I didn't take it, unsure what was happening.

He snapped out the barrel and showed me the magazine.

There were no bullets.

He closed it again and set it on the counter. "When

you came home after Christmas, I found it and removed the bullets."

I closed my eyes and felt the shame hit me hard. This entire time I thought I'd outsmarted him, but now I knew I never had a chance. He didn't flinch when the barrel was pressed to his temple because he knew there was no ammunition. He was testing me, seeing if I had the courage to actually pull the trigger.

And now he knew I didn't.

Tears formed under my eyelids and streaked down my cheeks. I didn't care that I gave in to my weakness, even in front of him. I felt stupid thinking I outsmarted this man when he outsmarted me a long time ago. I was doomed, trapped in this cage without walls. That was how powerful this man was. He could keep me there without chains or locks.

He cupped my cheeks and wiped my tears away with the pads of his thumbs.

I opened my eyes and saw him stare at me, his eyes softer than they were before. He kissed the corner of my mouth then ran his fingers through my hair. "I don't say this very often, but when I do, I mean it." He pressed his forehead to mine. "I'm sorry. I really am."

Also by Penelope Sky

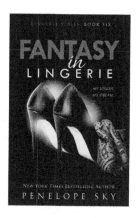

Bones is the son of the man who killed my aunt. He's the descendant of a psychopath, a murderer.

His handsome face, blue eyes, and strong physique can fool anyone into believing he's a good man.

Including me.

My loyalty to my family makes me despise him.

But I also can't stop thinking about him.

Thinking about his kiss.

Order Now